MR. MURDOCK
TAKES COMMAND

MR. MURDOCK
TAKES COMMAND

★

A Story of Pirates
and Rebellion in Haiti

By Joseph B. Icenhower, *Rear Admiral, U. S. N. (Ret.)*

ILLUSTRATED BY NORMAN GUTHRIE RUDOLPH

The John C. Winston Company

PHILADELPHIA • TORONTO

Other Books by the Author

MR. MIDSHIPMAN MURDOCK AND THE BARBARY PIRATES
SUBMARINE RENDEZVOUS
MAN AGAINST THE UNKNOWN
FIRST BOOK OF SUBMARINES
FIRST BOOK OF THE ANTARCTIC

ABOUT THE AUTHOR

JOSEPH BRYAN ICENHOWER was born in Parkersburg, West Virginia. He was appointed to the United States Naval Academy in 1932. His subsequent exploits are even more colorful than those of his fictional heroes, as he has seen action all over the world—in Europe, Panama, Peru, the Far East, the South Pacific, Tangier, Australia and New Zealand—as well as Haiti, which forms the background of his latest exciting adventure story.

He was commander of the submarine U. S. S. *Jallao* in World War II. Later, he commanded the only submarine ever to cross the Antarctic Circle as a unit of the Navy Task Force of the Byrd Antarctic Expedition in 1946–47. For conspicuous gallantry and outstanding skill while on active duty, the author was awarded several medals, including the Navy Cross, Silver Star Medal and Bronze Star Medal.

In 1954, Captain Icenhower became Commanding Officer of the Damage Control Training Center, in Philadelphia.

Now retired with the rank of rear admiral, Joseph B. Icenhower is engaged in private industry. He makes his home in Delaware County, Pennsylvania, with his wife and three boys.

CONTENTS

★

INTRODUCTION

THE United States Navy, during almost two hundred years of its life, has found its men involved in some rather complicated diplomatic situations. Few, if any, can compare with the complex political atmosphere in Hispaniola, or Haiti, at the turn of the nineteenth century.

Hispaniola, Jewel of the West Indies, was discovered by Columbus on his first voyage in 1492. That half of the island called Haiti was ceded by the Spanish to the French in 1697. Long a hangout for pirates and buccaneers, it had by the time of the American Revolution become France's richest colony. Its wealth, however, was based on slave labor, and disappeared overnight.

On the evening of the twenty-second of August, 1793, tom-toms throughout the island signaled a slave uprising. During the following week 800 plantations lay in ashes, their owners tortured, mutilated and dead. The leader of this uprising was a slave named Boukmann, who was killed within two weeks. On his death, another slave, Toussaint L'Ouverture, took command of the rebels and for the next ten years fought continuously. His trusted lieutenants were Jean Jacques Dessalines and Henri Christophe, both later to become Emperors of Haiti.

In Haiti, treason was a wholesale proposition. The whites on the island favored the King of France, who, unfortunately for them, was murdered by Paris mobs in 1793.

The mulattoes—freedmen and often plantation owners—
favored Republican France and fought the whites. During the first years of Haiti's existence, whites, blacks and
mulattoes were battling each other and the armies of
France in a decade of blood and confusion.

Toussaint eventually became dictator of Haiti and
thereby annoyed Napoleon, now supreme in France.
Napoleon backed a rebellion against Toussaint, spear-
headed by General Rigaud, then Governor of the Southern Province.

The United States at this time, while technically at
peace, was busy fighting an undeclared war at sea with
the French, with an occasional brush with the British.
More to embarrass Napoleon than for love of the black
government in Haiti, U. S. Navy ships were ordered to
aid Toussaint. Our aid reached sizeable proportions
when the U. S. S. *General Greene* shot up two of General
Rigaud's forts.

This book tells the story of a typical, self-sufficient midshipman of the period. The events and situation in Haiti
are based on historical fact. While the principal character
is purely fictional, he can be considered average for the
day. Although there are violence and cruelty in the book,
both are much tempered. The frightful and often incredible savagery of Haiti's history would not be credited
by most readers.

J. B. I.

MR. MURDOCK
TAKES COMMAND

★

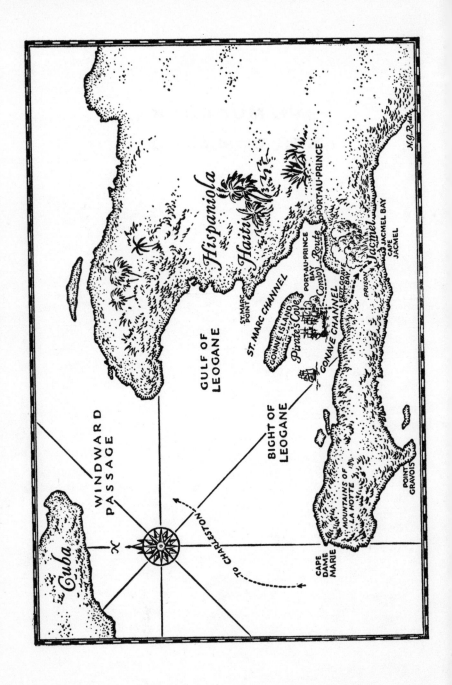

★

CHAPTER 1

The Victory

"CAPTAIN returning aboard, sir!" Mr. Midshipman Murdock called across the quarter-deck of the U. S. Schooner *Victory*. Lieutenant Rutledge, his white waistcoat unbuttoned and stock loosened against the noonday heat, walked slowly across the deck and stared balefully at the U. S. Frigate *Constitution*, riding at anchor some three hundred yards away.

"Perhaps I should say, 'hurrah!' eh, Jim?" the lieutenant growled. "If I did, t'would be far too feeble to be heard." He scowled at the figure of Captain Mellon climbing down the rope ladder over the frigate's side. "Call down to Knight. He's second in command of this hellship. Let him meet the old devil."

Jim walked over to the open hatch on the quarter-deck and called down the ladder. He heard Lieutenant Knight's "Very well," in answer, then turned and with an anxious sweep of his eyes took in every detail of the schooner's topside. The well-sanded white deck was spotless, the spars were perfectly aligned and the sails neatly furled.

"Have the men fall in at quarters, Jim." Lieutenant Knight, his tanned forehead glistening with perspiration, reached the deck. "Blast this heat!" he said, as he reluctantly buttoned his coat. "If it's this hot off Hispaniola in November, what must it be like in summer?" He

1

dabbed ineffectively at his sodden hatband, then set his hat squarely on his head.

"All hands to quarters!" Jim called forward.

The boatswain's mate passed the word below to the berth deck. Loungers on the gun deck hastened to their assigned positions, tidying their rumpled clothing as they fell in. Twelve marines, commanded by a boyish lieutenant and his red-faced sergeant, tramped heavily aft, with much creaking of leather and accouterments, to form a single line abaft the mainmast. In spite of the heat their uniforms were crisp, and their newly pipe-clayed crossbelts shone in the hot sun.

Jim took a position near the lee rail and ordered two seamen to rig a sea ladder. As officer of the deck, he was responsible for the ship's routine until relieved by the first lieutenant, a procedure that Lieutenant Knight did not seem inclined to follow at the moment.

Well forward on deck, he saw Dick Summers, the only other midshipman attached to the *Victory,* directing a party of seamen around the capstan. In all probability the captain's arrival on board would signal an order for getting underway. Jim noted with satisfaction that Dick would be prepared to heave short immediately.

Lieutenant Rutledge made a mocking bow to the midshipman. "I hasten to attend his highness' arrival," he said. Turning, he walked to the middle of the deck, then swung around to face the ladder.

Jim saw Lieutenant Knight move next to the other lieutenant and heard him speak in a low sharp voice.

"Easy, Randy," he cautioned. "There'll be the devil to pay if he doesn't find everything shipshape. Don't plague the captain today; he's not a well man."

"He's well enough to make life miserable for all hands aboard this dismal tub," grumbled Lieutenant Rutledge.

Lieutenant Knight glanced at the young midshipman who'd turned again to the rail, feigning no interest in the conversation he so obviously overheard. "Stow it!" he warned in an undertone. "You'll only make matters worse."

"Attention on deck!" shouted Jim, as he watched the gig ease in toward the ship's side. The seamen froze to attention, and the familiar slap of hand against musket was heard as the marines presented arms. He heard the gig bump ever so slightly against the schooner. Shortly, the scowling face of the commanding officer appeared over the lee rail. A moment later, he jumped to the deck and would have fallen had Jim not grabbed him by the arm.

Captain Mellon shook off the midshipman's hand petulantly. "I'm fully capable of walking my own deck, Mr. Murdock." He directed a churlish stare at the blushing young officer. Fully a head shorter than the eighteen-year-old Jim, his body was slight to the point of frailty. His face, red with the exertion of climbing the ladder, twitched nervously. Even as he stood, legs wide apart to meet the easy roll of the ship, he seemed to sway on his feet. Satisfied at length that he had put the young man in his place, he let his eyes wander forward to inspect the deck. Unable to find anything to complain about, he returned the officers' salutes, favored Lieutenant Rutledge with a look of utter disdain, then moved unsteadily toward his cabin.

Jim turned away from the uncomfortable glances of the other officers, leaned over the rail and ordered the gig to haul out. He turned again to the first lieutenant for orders.

"Have the crew fall out and hoist the boat in, Jim. I'll see if we have sailing orders." Lieutenant Knight turned and made for the captain's cabin.

After the men broke ranks to head for the nearest shade, Dick Summers hurried aft to the quarter-deck.

"What's the matter with the old curmudgeon, Jim?" he asked in a low voice.

"I don't know, Dick. He's so sick he can hardly stand on his feet, yet he won't give in to it and ask to be relieved. Sometimes I feel mighty sorry for him."

"Sorry!" grunted Dick. "He's been this way ever since we arrived on the West Indies station. What I can't understand is why Captain Talbot doesn't send him back home." He glanced across the radiantly blue water to the *Constitution,* rolling ponderously at anchor. "You'd think as commodore of the squadron he'd want able captains for his ships."

"I suspect the commodore has plenty on his mind trying to figure a way to stop the French privateers from capturing American merchantmen," Jim answered. "How would you like to cover the whole Caribbean with a handful of ships?"

"That's the commodore's problem," Dick replied. "Captain Mellon is ours."

"Come on, Dick, cheer up. We'll live through it."

Dick Summers raised his eyebrows skeptically. "You think so? Have you seen Hardy's back since the flogging?"

Jim nodded soberly and frowned. Hardy was a good seaman and an experienced helmsman. His big capable hands could hold the schooner on her course like no other helmsman aboard. Above average in intelligence, he'd foreseen a sudden blow and had dared suggest to the captain they take in canvas. The forestaysail carried away, even as the captain cursed him for an insubordinate dog. Raging, the officer assigned his helmsman twelve of the cat as punishment. Not even a combined appeal by all ship's officers could influence the captain to rescind his order, given in anger. Jim sensed a marked change in the attitude of the crew, perhaps not visible to an outsider but a difference recognized by every officer on board.

Jim's thoughts were interrupted by Lieutenant Knight's appearance on deck. He approached the two young officers, at the same time motioning Lieutenant Rutledge to join him.

"We're getting underway. Have the men take their stations, Jim; and, Dick, you heave the anchor to short stay. Randy, you make a signal to the flagship requesting permission to get underway then signal the convoy to form up astern of us."

"Where are we headed?" asked Lieutenant Rutledge.

"For action, I hope," replied the senior lieutenant grimly. "We're going to patrol off Jacmel."

"Jacmel!" Rutledge whistled. "General Rigaud's headquarters! This is news!"

It took but a very short time to get the schooner underway. At the cry, "Way aloft," the topmen scurried up the shrouds while the seamen on deck set first the jib to swing the ship's head slowly around, then the fore- and mainsail to catch a breeze so feeble it scarcely rippled the surface.

After being relieved of the deck by the sailing master, quiet, efficient Asa Dorr, Jim walked aft to the taffrail to stare reflectively along the lengthening wake. It was useless to go below, with the hot sun boiling the tar right out of the deck seams. He let his eyes wander over the green and brown terrain of the island astern. Hispaniola, Columbus' own land, he thought, the richest island in the Americas! Near the sea, the solid green of orderly canefields stretched away to the rugged mountains rising abruptly from the fertile plain some few miles in width. The dull brown of the mountains' lower slopes gave way

to the deep green of pine forests on forbidding heights.
Along the shore lay the toylike houses of Port-au-Prince,
all pink and white and lifeless in the hot sun.   There
were faint stirrings in the sleepy harbor itself, however, as
two brigs and three schooners, *Victory*'s convoy for the
trip, moved sluggishly after them in the torpid waters.

"They'll catch up with us if they have to row." A
voice at Jim's shoulder interrupted his thoughts.

Jim turned to see Lieutenant Rutledge behind him.
He watched the lieutenant lean against the taffrail and
survey the activity in the harbor with a sardonic grin.

"You'll never get one of those timid merchant skippers
to pass the island of Gonave without an escort," the older
man continued.

"Do you know how far we're to convoy them on their
way home, sir?" Jim asked.

"To the Bight of Léogane, I guess," said the other.
"Heard Knight say we'd see 'em clear of the island—at
least, them as can keep up.   They'll pick up a fair breeze
for the Windward Passage once clear of St. Marc Channel."   He took off his hat and ran his finely tapered fingers
through his dark wavy hair.   "Pretty island," he mused,
looking up at the high cool forests with longing.

"Just what I was thinking," remarked Jim.

"In this case the beauty is only on the surface.   I'd
sure hate to get caught in the back country alone."   He
grunted.   "Between the blacks, the whites and the mulattoes, they've invented some tortures that make our red
Indians look like saints."

"I thought General Toussaint had things pretty well
under control—except, of course, General Rigaud's
troops," said Jim.

"Don't be so naïve, Jim," Rutledge said.   "Toussaint

is about as good a general as they've ever seen around here, but he can't control Haiti."

"Don't you think Toussaint will get Rigaud?" asked Jim.

"Sure. He'll defeat him in no time," answered the lieutenant. "But what does he accomplish then? While he's south chasing Rigaud, one of his generals in the north will turn against him."

"Here's the thing that bothers me, sir," said Jim. "Won't the French send a fleet over here to help Rigaud now that we've been ordered to help Toussaint?"

"I doubt it. Napoleon has his hands full on the Continent."

"But Haiti was one of France's richest possessions. From what I've heard of Napoleon he won't take the slave uprising under Toussaint without a fight," said Jim.

"Indeed he won't," said the other. "The French will be here someday, once they whip the English." He spat over the rail in disgust. "Serves the fool French right. If they hadn't been screaming liberty, equality, and brotherhood all over the place and chopping each others' heads off at home, they'd have known what was going on over here."

"But Napoleon made Toussaint a general."

"Sure he did. He had to, because Toussaint was the real leader of the people. The French hope to hang onto Haiti, even if it means using the blacks to help them. There's no love between the two. Wait a few years, and you'll see the French swarming over the island like flies."

"In the meantime—"

"In the meantime," Rutledge broke in, "we go on helping a former black slave take the island from the French, who helped us get our freedom from the British."

"You don't think we ought to fight the French?" asked Jim.

"Of course we ought to fight them!" Rutledge snorted. "They started it by taking our merchantmen!" He looked at Jim sharply and in a lower voice added, "I hope we do get into action before old Mellon drives this crew to mutiny."

Jim looked up sharply. For the first time someone had actually spoken the ugly word. In his own mind he'd thought of the possibility. Someone else shared his views!

★

CHAPTER 2

Beat to Quarters

BY THE END of the afternoon watch, the lengthening shadows over the island of Gonave turned the green of the mountain slopes to deep purple. A freshening breeze heeled the *Victory* over under full-bellied sails that drove the sharp bow deep into each oncoming swell. Astern, the five ships under convoy filled away and scurried to a protected station off the starboard quarter of the Navy schooner. Given a steady breeze throughout the night, the convoy could expect to be clear of St. Marc Channel by dawn.

At midnight Jim came on deck for the midwatch, that usually quiet and uneventful tour of duty from midnight until four in the morning. In spite of the rigid Navy discipline, Jim always felt closer to his men during this watch. In the darkness the few men undoubtedly experienced a kinship and often spoke of their homes and their troubles. It was during these quiet watches that Jim had learned to respect the seaman Hardy. Hardy's quiet competence and his calm courage in difficult situations were admirable. This was why the captain's unjust punishment had such a tremendous impact on the crew. Jim had missed Hardy the past few nights, and his watch had seemed to lack its sharpness during the seaman's absence.

The night was clear and the holystoned deck shone in

the moonlight. Jim walked aft to check a screened white lantern on the stern, used as a guide light for the rest of the convoy. When he returned to the quarter-deck he was amazed to see Hardy step up to the helmsman, relieve him in a low voice, then give the helm an easy turn to get the feel of the ship. There was just enough light to outline the half-healed ugly stripes on the man's bare back.

For a brief moment Jim thought that life at sea for a sailor could often be worse than slavery. A quick feeling of compassion moved him to step up beside the man.

"Hardy, you're not fit for duty yet. Go below, I'll get someone to relieve you."

"Surgeon said I could come back to duty, sir," replied the tightlipped helmsman, the muscles rippling in his broad shoulders as he moved the helm slightly.

"But—"

"If you don't mind, sir, I'd rather be back up here." Hardy stared straight ahead into the darkness.

Jim studied the man thoughtfully. Perhaps it was better for him to be on deck. Certainly his back would feel better, and perhaps heal quicker in the warm breeze.

"Very well, Hardy," he answered, and turned his attention to the others of the watch. Noticing the younger seamen of the watch darting furtive looks at the older man's back and whispering among themselves, he found other duties for them forward.

During the four hours of his watch, his men were unusually silent. A couple of times Jim tried to draw Hardy into a conversation, without success. The helmsman stood a quiet efficient watch, but spoke only when spoken to. Several times Jim was prompted to express a word of encouragement or sympathy, but to do so would have been open criticism of the captain. Hardy's attitude made him uneasy, and once when he went forward to inspect the forepart of the ship, he returned to find several of the watch clustered around the helm, talking in undertones to Hardy. Jim was alarmed. Their furtive actions, as they broke up the gathering, led him to approach the helmsman warily.

"What were you talking about, Hardy?"

"The boys wanted to know how I felt, sir," Hardy replied.

Jim studied the impassive face carefully. He saw no trace of guile in the steady eyes. Perhaps he was unduly suspicious, he thought. Hardy looked too honest. He'd have a talk with him tomorrow anyway, he promised himself. Turning away he noticed a faint tinge of light in the east, time for Dick Summers to relieve him.

"What ho the watch, my boy?" Dick called out cheerily as he approached the quarter-deck.

"Convoy's all present," Jim answered with a wave toward the five shapes astern. "The course is east-northeast. Orders are to hold this course until clear of Gonave Island. That's it, to leeward." He eyed the dark bulk of the island some five miles away. "Keep the convoy closed up. Rigaud's barges raiding from the island took a brig here in St. Marc's Channel last week. I heard Lieutenant Knight say Rigaud had about forty barges and some fifteen hundred men operating against our shipping along the coast." He looked up at the sea of canvas above the ship. "We had fresh breezes until about an hour ago, but they're dying away fast. I doubt if we're making more than two knots."

"Right," said Dick. "I'll take over."

Jim moved toward the lee rail and motioned Dick to follow. In a few words he outlined the suspicious actions of his watch. "How about keeping your eyes open to see if your men act strangely."

Dick nodded soberly. "I'll keep an eye on them," he promised. "Now you go ahead and get some sleep."

Sleep didn't come as quickly as it usually did for Jim after a long watch. He couldn't get rid of his uneasy feeling. His thoughts went back to the gathering of seamen around the helm. He'd better have a talk with Lieutenant Knight, too, in the morning.

When Jim finally fell asleep he had the sensation of just having dozed when the sound of running feet on the deck above snapped him wide awake.

In a flash he was out of his bunk throwing his clothes on. He heard the muffled roll of drums. Beat to quarters! Rigaud's barges must be attacking the convoy, he thought, as he ran topside.

The early morning sun blinded him momentarily when he reached the weather deck. A quick glance at the sails showed him the *Victory* was becalmed. Running forward, his practiced eye noticed every detail of the gun crews' activity. The Navy schooner carried fourteen large guns, ten 6-pounders and four 4-pounders. Jim commanded the starboard guns and Dick Summers the port battery. Evidently Summers had been relieved of the watch, because Jim saw him hurrying from gun to gun on the portside. The two boys attached to Jim's battery ran forward, their leather aprons filled with cartridges.

"Load with grape!" Lieutenant Knight bellowed the order from the quarter-deck.

Gun captains opened their ports, shotted and ran out their guns, the crews straining as they hauled on the gun tackle. While the gunners were busy priming, Jim saw that the tubs alongside each gun were filled with salt water.

As each of the gun captains finished his priming, he picked up a slow match and held it, waiting for the order to light up. Satisfied his battery was ready for action, Jim walked forward where two seamen were rigging a swivel gun, close by the bow of the ship. He watched them lower the oarlock-shaped pivot into a sturdy stock in the rail, then check it by swinging it right and left. Loading it with a powder cartridge and a handful of musket balls, they reported ready to the midshipman.

Jim nodded approvingly. The small bore cannon could raise havoc among massed men in a close-in fight and could be loaded much more rapidly than the larger carriage guns.

With everything under control, Jim for the first time moved over alongside Dick Summers.

"Where's the enemy, Dick?" he asked.

Summers pointed astern. "Barges. Eleven of 'em at the last count. There behind the convoy." His face showed deep concern. "We'll have a tough time protecting all the merchant ships in this calm," he added.

Jim leaned over the rail to look aft.

"Good Lord! Which of our ships is that so far astern?"

"The brig *Mary*," growled Summers. "I signaled her three times since sunrise to close up, but her mutton-headed imbecile of a skipper wouldn't pay any attention." He moved closer to Jim and muttered in his ear. "Now the old man blames me for not keeping the convoy together. Right in front of my own watch he called me an incompetent blunderer." The midshipman, his face grim with suppressed anger at the memory, glowered at the quarter-deck where Captain Mellon ran frantically from one side of the ship to the other.

Jim jumped to the rail, grabbed the foremast shrouds and leaned out over the sea for a better look astern. Except for the *Mary*, the convoy was fairly well closed up. She had fallen well astern and was directly in line with the squat hulls of the wide-beamed barges approaching from the rear. It appeared that the *Mary*'s skipper was anxious to atone for his former laxity, because Jim observed two long sweeps projecting from each side of the brig. That the crew was badly frightened was evident from the clumsy and unco-ordinated efforts of the rowers.

Still further astern, but moving up fast, Rigaud's pirates were closing in on the brig. They were less than two miles distant, and each boat appeared to be overflowing with a mass of humanity. Propelled by at least twenty oarsmen, each carried a cannon mounted in the bow. There was no doubt that they were headed for the *Mary*, and even less doubt that they would overtake her before she reached the protection of the *Victory*. Even as the other ships watched the race, the captain of the brig arrived at the same conclusion. His longboat swung out and was quickly lowered to the water. The crew tumbled over the side and pulled madly for the *Victory*, leaving their ill-fated ship to the approaching hordes.

Only one barge stopped at the abandoned *Mary*, and just long enough to send a few men aboard to take possession. The other barges drove on toward the next nearest vessel, the *Rover*, a brig from Baltimore. They were close enough now for Jim to see there were at least fifty men in each craft. A puff of smoke billowed out from the side of the *Rover* signaling to the convoy that her captain was no coward. The crew of the *Victory* cheered the brig's gallant action as a geyser of water erupted just ahead of the leading barge.

"Rig the sweeps, port and starboard!"

The watching men jumped at the sharp order. The gun crews hastily broke out the long oars and rigged them through the small ports between the guns. With two men straining at each sweep, the *Victory* turned slowly and gathered headway.

The barges were closing fast. Jim doubted they could reach the *Rover* in time. Suddenly it occurred to him they might be able to reach the barges with the forward 6-pounders. Running aft to the quarter-deck he found Captain Mellon ranging from one side of the deck to the other, cursing first the convoy, then the sluggish headway of his own ship.

"Sir," Jim said. "Request permission to draw the grapeshot and load round in the forward two guns for a go at the enemy. I think—"

"Silence!" screamed the captain. He stared popeyed at the midshipman. "You would tell me how to fight my ship?"

"But, sir—"

"Get back to your station, you insolent puppy!" The captain's face working with emotion, he took a step forward as if he would strike his junior officer. "Get back to your guns, Mr. Murdock, or I'll put you under arrest!" His voice rose to a half-hysterical pitch.

Jim's bewilderment changed to one of cold rage as he saluted, wheeled sharply and returned to his battery. He was conscious of the amazed stares of the gun crews as they looked first at him and then at the quarter-deck.

Dick Summers walked over to his side and muttered, "I honestly believe he's crazy, Jim. Why the devil doesn't Lieutenant Knight take over?" He turned to glower at the captain then quickly nudged Jim. "Maybe he will! Look aft!"

Jim glanced toward the quarter-deck to see the first lieutenant talking earnestly to the captain, and apparently speaking his mind, for the commanding officer stood spellbound, an incredulous look on his face. Without giving the older man a chance to speak, the lieutenant spun on his heel and walked forward to the two midshipmen.

"Draw the grape from your forward two guns and load with round shot, Jim." His eyes met Jim's steadily. "I don't have to tell you I want you to hole one of those barges. A lot may depend on it." Seeing that Jim understood the situation he continued, "I'll swing the ship enough for the guns to bear. Good luck!" He turned and hurried back to the quarter-deck.

Under Jim's watchful eye the gunners trained the carriages as far forward as possible, grunting as they levered the heavy gun with handspikes. He checked the loading with care, and let the fine-mealed priming powder run through his fingers before priming the touchhole. He determined to get a hit and prove the captain wrong.

As the *Victory* came slowly to port, he laid his number one gun with care. He reached for the slow match, held his breath and waited for the ship to swing left. With agonizing slowness she came around. Behind him the rest of the crew watched, tense and silent.

As the gun barrel lined up with the barge nearest the *Rover,* Jim made a catlike leap to one side to avoid the recoil, and dropped the end of the glowing match onto the touchhole. The gun jumped in its tackle and recoiled with a snap of the breechings. Jim darted a look over the rail in time to see a splash just short and to the right of the enemy. He ducked down again and laid the second gun. The first had been a good sighting shot; he felt confident about this one.

Even before the smoke had cleared sufficiently for him to see the results, he knew it was a hit because the gun crews farther aft cheered and slapped each other on the back. Soon after, he saw the barge, one side shattered, wallowing in the oily swell as its motley crew of whites, blacks and mulattoes spilled into the sea.

Jim watched the brig *Rover* put up a desperate fight with her feeble battery against the other barges. Unfortunately, the gallant defense was quickly overwhelmed as hordes of screaming pirates swarmed over the brig's side to cut down the meager crew. A groan sounded along the deck of the *Victory* as a huge pirate slashed away the merchantman's colors with a sweep of his machete.

He could see that the pirates had no intention of defending the *Rover* against the slowly approaching *Victory*. Two of the barges swept out ahead of the ship. They hastily rigged a towline to the brig's bow, then took up a fast stroke. Five more barges approached the *Victory* warily. They meant to attack her and prevent recovery of the stolen prize.

In very short order Jim had little to think about save defense of his own ship. The bow cannon on the barges sent one screaming shot after the other into the Navy schooner. The more maneuverable barges kept their approach bow on to prevent the Navy broadsides from bearing. Fortunately, the *Victory* had just enough way on to permit the sailing master to unmask the guns on the starboard side.

"Fire as you bear!" Lieutenant Knight's voice roared down the deck.

One by one the guns of Jim's battery boomed a lethal salute to the enemy. When the smoke cleared, one barge had been holed, and as evidenced by the confusion and cries in two others, the grapeshot had caused severe casualties. The pirates weren't eager for more and backed quickly away. When well clear, they huddled together for a council of war.

The *Victory* lost no time in manning the sweeps once

again to get the becalmed vessel underway for the *Rover,*
now fast drawing clear of the convoy. The two barges
renewed their towing with frantic haste, having seen the
effect of the Navy schooner's broadsides. Jim walked
up and down the deck encouraging the men on. Unless
they could move faster they would never rescue the cap-
tive brig.

"Look, Jim!" yelled Summers. "Look aft!"

Jim turned quickly to look out over the oily sea. Not
five hundred yards astern he saw a few cat's-paws rippling
the surface. A wind!

"That's all we need!" cried Jim. "Give us a decent
breeze and this fight will be over!"

Jim watched anxiously as the ripples overtook the
ship. The sails flapped gently and the vessel stirred with
new life.

There were other anxious eyes watching the faint
breeze. The barges, no longer indecisive, realized they
must attack soon if they were to retain their advantage.
Re-forming, they again made for the *Victory,* driving toward her with all the speed they could muster. One by
one their cannon roared.

Again the *Victory*'s broadside drove the pirates away
with the loss of one barge. This time the enemy had
enough. Splitting up their force, two barges headed for
the *Mary,* now well astern, and the others made for the
Rover, their oars churning the water as they raced to prevent the ship's recapture.

Jim felt the *Victory* heel over slightly. Glancing aloft,
he saw the sails belly out in the freshening breeze. We'll
get the *Rover* back now, he thought grimly. Turning, he
ordered the forward guns to load with round shot. Just
give him a chance at those two barges towing her!

His next shot turned the tide of battle. A clean hole in the first of the two barges towing the *Rover* put an end to the pirates' hope of getting her clear. The remaining barge cut her towline in panic and headed for the safety of the island's reef.

The *Victory,* once again lively under all sails, let go a broadside to rake the *Rover*'s deck, still swarming with pirates. The havoc was frightful as the shot cut down the stranded men. It took but one raking broadside to force the disorganized horde to surrender. One pirate ran aft and ran up the *Rover*'s colors again.

Within minutes the *Victory* was alongside, and, while the two vessels were lashed together, the surviving cutthroats were herded forward under the menacing guns of the marines. Inspection of the ship showed tragic evidence of stiff resistance by the American merchant skipper and his small crew. All were dead.

The *Rover* had suffered no damage to hull or rigging that couldn't be repaired in a short time. With the convoy standing by, Captain Mellon sent a repair party aboard to make her shipshape, while the remainder of the crew turned to on repairs to the *Victory.* The *Mary* was the convoy's only loss. Jim watched her sail away, her pirate crew having taken advantage of the *Victory*'s battle to get clear. Captain Mellon would not leave his convoy to try to recapture her.

By midday the damage to the *Rover* was repaired. Jim was on his way to his cabin when a seaman saluted him and told him the captain wanted to see him. He approached the quarter-deck with a sinking heart. Here's another tongue lashing, he thought, as he moved wearily aft.

Anyone with half an eye could see the captain was

barely able to stand. His narrow face was drawn and white with fatigue. Even so, the look he threw at Jim as he approached was full of malevolence.

He waited until Jim saluted, then growled, "Think you can handle the brig, Murdock?"

Jim was so surprised at the question he could only gape as it dawned on him that he was being offered command of the *Rover* as a prize ship.

"Well, speak up! Don't stand there like a clod," hissed the captain. "Aren't you capable of ordinary seamanship?"

"Yes—yes, sir," stammered Jim.

★

CHAPTER 3

CAPTAIN Murdock

JIM discovered the brig to be a well-found craft. The sails were virtually new and the rigging had been recently tarred. Signs of a former competent skipper were everywhere. Now that all the damage was repaired, he couldn't help but feel possessive as he walked forward on the deck—*his* deck, he thought proudly. Two marine sentries were guarding a hatch, its grating lashed securely in place.

"How many prisoners are below?" he asked.

"We counted forty, sir," one of the marines answered, "and if you don't mind my saying so, they're a scurvy lot."

"He's right, Mr. Murdock," the other marine spoke up. "Them heathen'll take a heap of watchin'."

"I'm sure they will," replied Jim. He glanced at the quarter-deck of the *Victory*. The two ships were still lashed together; however, the last of the repair party was leaving the brig and it was time to go aboard to assemble his prize crew. Although infinitely happy with his new command, he was a bit uneasy about the prisoners below. He had hoped the *Victory* would take them aboard, but Captain Mellon proved adamant. "Ain't going to stink up my ship with a load of scum," he'd said. He did intend for the *Rover* to follow the *Victory* to Jacmel, and there try to exchange the prisoners for any American seamen held in captivity by Rigaud. Oh well, Jim thought,

21

it wouldn't take too long to get to Jacmel, then he would
be free to head for a port when the brig could be properly
condemned for legal sale.   He dismissed his uneasiness
and returned to the *Victory*.

Captain Mellon was below decks, but Jim found
Lieutenant Knight on the quarter-deck.

"How's the brig, Jim?" asked the first lieutenant.

"She's a trim craft, sir," replied Jim enthusiastically.
"I'll be ready to sail as soon as I get a crew aboard."

Lieutenant Knight faced the young officer with a look
of concern.   "Jim, I hate to tell you this, but the captain
says you're to take only four men."

"Four men!" gasped the midshipman.   "Great guns,
sir, I can't even handle her sails with so few hands."   Jim
stared at the first lieutenant in amazement.   "Surely you're
mistaken, sir."

"I wish I were, Jim," said the other gravely.   "I tried
to reason with the captain, but he expects you to detail
a party of the prisoners to do the work and your men will
only have to watch them.   He pointed out that this is
common procedure in returning a prize to port."

"I know, sir," Jim pleaded, "but this is no common
prize.   Those men aren't merchant seamen, they're a
bunch of villainous cutthroats."   His jaw set in anger.
"I'm going down and talk to him, sir.   Surely he can see
the wrong of it!"

"Don't, Jim!"   Lieutenant Knight held the young
officer by the arm.   "If you go down there and try to talk
to him he'll take the command away from you."   He drew
the midshipman back to his side.   "This is the opportunity you've waited for so long.   Don't give the captain the
pleasure of taking the ship away from you.   He could
wreck your career."   Jim sighed.   Lieutenant Knight continued: "Now look, you won't need more than ten

prisoners on deck at most. We'll be off Jacmel in three days, where you'll get rid of the lot of them. If we don't pick up any American prisoners to give you a hand, I'll see that you get a few more men from the *Victory*."

"But, sir—" Jim started to protest.

"I know it's unfair, Jim, but you stay close astern of us. We'll keep our eyes on you. I doubt if the prisoners will try anything with us so close."

"Well," Jim replied in a doubtful voice, "I'll give it a try." He looked at the lieutenant with a grin. "May I pick my own crew, or has the captain decided who I'm to take?"

Lieutenant Knight grinned back and glanced toward the quarter-deck hatch. "Yes, you may select them, but I'd advise you to hurry. I'll cast you off as soon as you have your men aboard."

Jim had already given some thought to the crew he'd need. Now the selection was of even greater significance. He had already decided on John Barnum, the quartermaster of his watch, and Jeb Hews and James Burke, two gunners of his battery. He debated for some time on the fourth man, then picked Hardy. If the man was pleased he didn't show it. He quietly packed his sea bag and appeared topside with the others.

The quartermaster carried a spare sextant, and the gunners, Jim was pleased to note, each carried a powder horn of fine-grained French priming powder; all four carried boarding cutlasses and tomahawks.

Knight looked startled when he saw Hardy standing with the prize crew. He drew Jim aside and said, "Why are you taking Hardy? After what you told me earlier today about the watch last night, don't you think you're taking a risk?"

Jim glanced at the seaman. "I don't think so. Hardy's

a good man basically, I'm sure. He'll be better off away from the *Victory*. Anyway, he can't cause any trouble with the other three; I'd stake my life on them."

"Very well, Jim. It's your decision," Knight said. "I hope you're right. Now get aboard, and I'll cast you off before the captain comes topside."

"Aye, sir, and thanks," replied Jim. He turned, ordered the prize crew to board their new ship and followed them over the rail to the deck of the *Rover*.

The new captain had little time in the next hour to reflect on his elevated position. As soon as the two marines jumped back aboard the schooner, Jim stuck two pistols in his belt, put Hardy on the helm and led the other three sailors forward to get some canvas on the ship. With the courses set, he felt the brig pick up steerageway.

Satisfied they could keep up with the *Victory*, he had Hews cut the lashing on the grating over the hatch. Between them they slid it to one side, then Jim stood at the top of the ladder, both pistols in hand.

"Send your captain on deck," he ordered the sea of upturned faces below him.

He heard a confused babble of sound that dwindled then died out as a swarthy face appeared at the hatch coaming. Jim motioned the man to come on deck. Nimbly and with no outward sign of fear, a rather small but well-proportioned mulatto ran up the ladder. He made a half-mocking bow to the young officer and murmured, "Your servant, sir."

"What's your name?" the midshipman asked.

"Capitaine Antoine Cruet, at your service, m'sieu." The man's smile did not mask the contempt in his eyes as he saw the small size of the prize crew.

"You understand we could hang you and your entire crew for piracy?" Jim said.

The man raised his eyes in feigned astonishment. "Piracy, mon capitaine? But no, mon capitaine. We sail under the letter of marque from his excellency, le Général Rigaud, Governor of the Southern Province." He shook his head from side to side. "No, m'sieu, we are not pirates. Here." He reached inside his dirty shirt and withdrew a soiled and greasy paper which he offered to the midshipman.

Jim waved the paper aside. "Look, Cruet, you and I both know your letter of marque isn't worth the paper it's written on." He studied the man carefully. "You do have a chance of gaining your freedom, however."

The pirate's eyes flickered with interest, although his face remained expressionless.

"You call up your ten best seamen," Jim directed. "If they behave themselves and take orders as proper hands, we'll make every effort to exchange the lot of you for any Americans in Jacmel."

"M'sieu le capitaine is most gracious," answered Cruet with a deep bow. "You have my word of honor as a Frenchman. I give you my parole, m'sieu." He spread his hands theatrically. "I, Antoine Cruet, pledge my honor that you will find no fault with my men." He turned to the hatchway and rolled off a list of ten names in quick succession.

When the ten men summoned by their captain appeared on deck, he had them form a rough line facing the young midshipman.

Jim reckoned he'd never seen a more villainous gang of cutthroats in his life. By comparison the Barbary pirates of the Mediterranean would have appeared positively angelic. Rigaud must have swept every filthy port of the Indies to get this crew. Burke and Barnum took a firmer grasp on their cutlasses as they surveyed the row of mixed renegade French and mulattoes that stood before them. There was but one pure Negro in the group.

"Have them turn around," Jim ordered the swarthy captain.

Obviously puzzled, Cruet nonetheless complied.

"Now tell them the first one that moves gets a pistol ball through his head."

"But, m'sieu—"

"Do as you are told, then join the line yourself," Jim ordered in a steely voice.

In rapid Creole, Cruet complied. Jim watched the men as they stared straight ahead toward the bow of the ship.

"The two swivel guns on the quarter-deck are trained directly on your backs, Cruet. I suggest you emphasize to your men the danger in turning their heads."

"Oui, m'sieu," the other answered quickly, some of his former confidence shaken. This babe of a midshipman was proving difficult.

Jim motioned Burke and Barnum to turn the two men on one end of the line around. Motioning them aft, he marched the two at pistol point to the open hatch just forward of the helm. In his previous inspection of the brig he had discovered this empty stowage space which now suited his plan admirably. He motioned the two below.

Jim repeated the silent maneuver, two men at a time, until only Cruet remained forward on deck; then he walked up behind him and said quietly, "You may turn around now, Captain."

Cruet turned, his eyes darting around the deck for signs of his men. "But where—" he stammered, nonplused.

"In the hold, my friend, where I now intend to put

you," Jim snapped. "You don't think I'm going to let you and ten of your most loyal men have the freedom of my deck, do you?"

Cruet's dark eyes met the level gaze of the young officer. "M'sieu le capitaine is veree clevaire." His lips curled in a sneer. "You will go far, mon capitaine, if you live long enough." Without another word he walked swiftly aft and dropped through the open hatchway. The quartermaster slid the grating in place, lashed it securely, then joined Jim at the forward hatch.

Jim called down into the forward hold: "I want ten seamen on deck. All blacks. No blancs or men of color!"

Slowly at first, then more rapidly as those below saw the leaders reach the deck unharmed, ten men crawled out of the hatchway.

Jim lined them up and looked them over carefully. "Which one of you speaks English?" he asked.

"I does." A big Negro with a scar on one cheek spoke up.

"Tell your friends they must obey orders instantly. Give us no trouble and we'll see you reach land again. One mutinous move and you'll be shot on the spot. Do you understand?"

The Negro nodded.

"You'll be their bo'sun. You relay orders to them. If they do their work they have nothing to fear." Jim looked aloft. "I want the royals and the gallants set. Get to work!"

Whether it was fear or the hope of eventual freedom that drove them, Jim could not complain of his forced crew. Convinced of their ability to handle the sails, he left Hews and Burke in charge and walked back to the helm. Barnum looked at him with unfeigned admiration as he approached.

"Mr. Murdock," he said hesitantly, "if you don't mind my sayin' so, that was about the sharpest bit o' handlin' prisoners I ever seen."

"Thank you, Barnum," said Jim, a bit embarrassed. He glanced quickly at Hardy, and somehow felt deflated when the helmsman made no comment but looked straight ahead. He told himself he wanted no spoken approval from the man but he could at least have looked in his direction. The old uneasiness of the night before returned. Blast it! *He* hadn't punished the man. He turned and stared up ahead at the *Victory*. She had drawn ahead slightly. Glancing aloft he noted the prisoners setting the sails he'd ordered. With more canvas they'd catch up.

"Keep her well closed up on the lee quarter, Hardy," he ordered.

"Aye, sir. Well closed up on the lee quarter," repeated the helmsman.

Jim turned to Barnum. "I'm going below to the captain's cabin and have a look around. Call me instantly if you need me."

"I will that, Mr. Murdock," answered the quartermaster.

Jim found the captain's cabin in a complete state of confusion. The pirates, during their brief stay aboard, had made a hurried search for anything of value. Unable to make off with their loot, they had left most of it piled on the cabin deck. Jim found an odd assortment of trade goods, including gaudy bandannas, several small kegs of priming powder, and various other trinkets to catch the natives' eyes. The looters had ripped the mattress off the captain's bunk, and the midshipman saw to his surprise three fishnets and a dozen boxes of shiny fishhooks.

Captain's private stock, he thought. Ought to get a pretty penny for those fishhooks anywhere in the Indies.

In racks along the bulkheads there were two large-caliber blunderbusses of ancient vintage. They must have really been in a hurry to overlook those, he thought. With the two swivel guns already on deck and the four 4-pounder carriage guns, the brig could be well defended by a determined crew.

Satisfied at length with his inspection, he returned to the weather deck. A quick look forward assured him the blacks were well under control. Both Hews and Burke hovered near the swivel guns. Hardy stood at the helm, his sturdy body swaying to the movement of the ship. Barnum paced the deck near the helm, his keen eyes on every movement of the impressed crew.

Jim joined the quartermaster. "Barnum, we'll have to provide food and water for the prisoners. We can't let them on deck today, but perhaps tomorrow we can let them topside a few at a time. We'll feed our deck hands first, then let the black bo'sun take rations below to the others." He paused and looked his four men over. "After that we'll divide into two watches. I'll take Hardy, and you take Hews and Burke for your watch."

"Aye, sir," replied the quartermaster.

Jim let his eyes wander over the small carriage guns. It would require the combined exertions of all four men to serve the guns, and no one could be spared in action to make trips below. He'd better get some powder up from the magazine. He planned to put all of the black seamen in the hold in the event of action, and although he could not believe that Captain Mellon would expect him to be much help in a fight, he determined to fight the ship if the occasion came up.

About four in the afternoon, Jim told the prisoners on deck to leave their work.   He had them gather aft to sit down in a semicircle, with their backs to the helm. Seated, they were less likely to make trouble and would constantly be under the watchful eyes of the Americans on the quarter-deck.

At sunset the *Victory* rigged a shielded stern light for the convoy to steer by.   The evening was clear, the breeze held, and all the ships were well clear of St. Marc's Channel by midnight.   Jim noted with satisfaction the manner in which the group kept closed up after the attack.   According to plan, the merchant vessels would leave the convoy at daybreak, to head north for the Windward Passage and home, while the two Navy vessels would head west and round Cape Dame Marie for Jacmel.

Shortly after dawn the *Victory* made a sharp turn to the left, the *Rover* following closely in her wake.   The merchantmen dipped their colors in salute as the convoy separated.   Jim ran aft to dip his colors and noted happily that he beat the *Victory* in answering the salute.   The brig was well within the distance ordered, and Jim could clearly see the deck watch on the schooner ahead.   He watched Captain Mellon walk aft to look the brig over. Instinctively Jim's eyes checked the set of his sails.   They were drawing well, and he doubted if the captain could find fault.   Whatever his superior's thoughts might be, they were undoubtedly interrupted by a cry of "Sail ho!" from the foretop of the *Victory*. The cry was plainly heard aboard the brig.

Jim glanced around the horizon, but could see only the sails of their former convoy, now hull down to the north.

"Burke," he called to the gunner, "go aloft and see if you can make out a sail."

Burke ran quickly to the shrouds and hurried aloft.
"Sail, sir!" he called down after a moment's study of
the horizon. "Schooner-rigged, she is, about the size of
the *Victory*."

At the same instant Barnum called the midshipman's
attention to a string of signals on the *Victory*.

"Make chase," Jim said. "Guess we'll have to push
her now, Hardy." He called up to Burke, "Lay below,
Burke!"

Burke hurried down to the deck and reported. "She's
on about the same course we're on, Mr. Murdock. It'll
take us all day to overhaul her, if she doesn't come about."

The gunner's prediction proved a correct one.
Throughout the day the two ships gave chase to the
stranger. There being little else for the brig to do but
keep up with the Navy schooner, Jim turned his impressed seamen to, on deck. He detailed one for galley
duty and had him cook up a mess of junk, or salt beef,
for the prisoners.

Thinking he might learn something of the fighting on
the mainland, he called Antoine Cruet on deck to ply
him with questions. The swarthy pirate captain proved
singularly lacking in knowledge of his superior's actions.
Jim attributed this to the fact of Cruet having been on
Gonave for the past two months. The captain seemed
particularly co-operative, and his change in character struck
the young midshipman as being too sudden. His meek
and mild manner didn't jibe with his arrogance of the
day before. Jim expected him to demand more food and
water and generally be unpleasant. He made a mental
note to keep a close watch on the grating after dark. For
the moment he contented himself with sending Hardy,
who'd been relieved of the helm by Barnum, to the lower
deck with orders to check the forward and after bulkheads

of each hold. Hardy evidently made a thorough inspection, considering the time he took to make it; consequently Jim breathed a little easier when he reported all secure below.

In the late afternoon *Victory* fired a warning gun for the strange schooner to haul up into the wind. The chase ignored it as she did several others fired at intervals. By sunset the two American vessels had closed enough so that the stranger's colors could be identified. Although they were Danish and therefore neutral, Jim realized this could mean little, since ships usually hoisted neutral colors in wartime as a ruse or precaution.

It was only when one of the *Victory*'s guns laid a shot close aboard that the strange schooner came up into the wind. Although the sun had set, there was sufficient light to observe a few men on deck of the low-lying schooner. Jim thought with a chuckle that the skipper was in for a bad time for leading Captain Mellon such a merry chase.

Anyone with half an eye could see why she was able to prolong the chase. Although not quite as large as the *Victory*, she had very sharp lines for a merchantman.

The rows of dancing lights on the deck of the *Victory* made Jim realize Captain Mellon was taking no chances; the gunners' slow matches were lighted and ready. Jim called Hews and Burke to his side and ordered them to load their four small carriage guns. He'd better be as prepared as he could be; anyway the loading would familiarize the gunners with the guns.

The *Victory* had a small boat in the water; evidently Captain Mellon intended to send a boarding party to minutely inspect the stranger. It seemed to crawl across the choppy water in the fast-growing darkness. Hews and Burke had all four guns loaded and run out before the boat reached the other ship.

Suddenly a sheet of flame enveloped the side of the stranger; the deep boom of a broadside rolled over the sea. Jim stood aghast as the *Victory*'s mainmast shuddered, then came crashing down. Powder on her deck ignited with a flash that revealed broken bulwarks on one side. Caught by complete surprise, *Victory*'s answering broadside was ragged and uneven. Even above the confused noise on the ship's deck ahead, Jim could hear Captain Mellon screaming orders.

"Man those port guns!" yelled Jim to his gunners. Sick with apprehension over the fate of his shipmates, he turned to Hardy. "Bring her to starboard quick. Run in close alongside the chase. Those popguns of ours will do some damage!"

"Oui, mon capitaine, but not to our friends on the *Tres Amis*," a voice behind him murmured.

Dragging frantically at the pistols in his belt, Jim whirled just in time to miss taking a smashing blow. Instead, the club shaved his head to send a searing pain through his shoulder as it knocked him to his knees. He shook his head to clear the red haze before his eyes, then found himself jerked to his feet by two pirates who twisted him around to face the gloating Captain Cruet.

"Ah, m'sieu. The shoe, she is on the other feet, no?" He sneered, then turned to his crew. "And now, mes enfants, a kiss for the américain ship before we leave."

Growling their approval, the pirates swarmed to the carriage guns and the smaller swivels on the afterdeck.

"No!" cried Jim, struggling in the arms of two pirates. He looked around the deck for his crew. Poor Hews and Burke were lying deathly still alongside the cannon, Barnum sat in front of the helm holding his head, the blood running through his fingers. Jim's eyes searched in vain for Hardy. Probably tossed him overboard, he thought.

Jim knew any further struggling on his part would bring the club smashing down on his head. He stood still and racked his brain for some sort of action to take. If only he could warn the *Victory!* He determined to wait until Cruet had the *Rover* close aboard, then yell a warning.

As if reading his mind, the crafty captain made a motion to one of his crew just as the *Rover* approached the stern of the schooner. Jim struggled desperately but couldn't prevent the man from stuffing a rag in his mouth. He was helpless against the combined strength of three husky pirates.

Horror-struck, he watched the *Rover* move quietly up alongside the *Victory,* no more than fifty feet of water separating the two ships. Just as the *Rover's* bow passed the Navy schooner's stern, he saw the figure of a man run to the rail of the larger vessel, then heard Captain Mellon's hysterical scream.

"Murdock, are you crazy? Keep clear and give me sea room, you blasted idiot!"

"Boom!" The *Rover's* 4-pounders and two swivel guns blazed away at the unsuspecting schooner.

Jim saw Captain Mellon clutch his shoulder in anguish and heard him scream, "Murdock, I'll have you hanged for this!"

The young midshipman struggled in blind rage against his captors. Through tear-glazed eyes he watched the black helmsman put the helm hard over to swing the *Rover* clear. His tortured ears could still hear the insane screaming of his captain as the brig disappeared into the night.

★

CHAPTER 4

Treachery

JIM woke with a spinning head that refused to come out of a spin. When he tried to raise a hand to his forehead, he saw that both wrists were manacled. A short chain, its other end fastened to a ringbolt in the ship's hull, permitted him but little movement. He remembered the pirates throwing him into the hold, but after that, all was blank. Sitting up as best he could, he strained his eyes in the darkness. Beneath the hold deck he could hear bilge water gurgle with each roll of the ship. He moved one foot and heard a rat scurry away.

Slowly his eyes began to focus and accustom themselves to the darkness. He could make out two inert figures in the hold with him.

"Hews!" he called. "Wake up, Hews!"

One of the figures stirred, groaned, and sat up.

"Is that you, Hews?" Jim asked.

"Aye, sir," mumbled the sailor. "What's left of me."

"How badly are you hurt?" Jim asked anxiously.

"I don't rightly know, Mr. Murdock," the other answered.

Jim watched him flex his arms, then run his hands all over his body.

"Don't think anything's broke, sir." Hews rubbed the back of his head. " 'Ceptin' maybe my head's broke, the way it feels."

35

"Is that Barnum next to you?"

Hews rolled over and stared at the apparently lifeless figure sprawled on the deck by his side.

"Yes, sir, I reckon so, 'cause Burke's dead. I saw 'em throw him over the side." He prodded Barnum with his toe. A protesting groan was the only answer he could get. "At least he ain't dead yet, Mr. Murdock," he offered. He kicked the other sailor a little harder. "Hey, Barnum! Wake up!"

Slowly, Barnum, with many groans, rolled over to a sitting position. He stared dully around the darkened hold, his eyes finally coming to rest on Jim.

"Are you badly hurt, Barnum?" the midshipman asked.

The sailor continued to stare at the young officer in a daze. Finally he said thickly, "Is that you, Mr. Murdock?"

"Yes," said Jim, his voice betraying his anxiety. "Tell me, are you badly hurt?"

Barnum started to raise his left arm, then dropped it back to the deck with a cry of pain. "My arm, sir," he groaned, "I reckon she's broke."

"Let it rest against your body," Jim cautioned. "Don't move any more than you have to until I can get a look at it. I'll try to get someone down here." He glanced up at the deck grating above him. Only a few tiny shafts of light filtered through. "Hey! On deck!" he shouted.

Although he could hear men moving about on the deck above him, no one came to the grating. Jim raised his voice in a louder shout. "Cruet, send someone down here!"

Still no one came to the covered opening.

The midshipman jerked savagely at the chains holding his wrists. The iron bit deeply into his flesh. He winced with pain and forced himself to relax. He couldn't fight the impossible; those bolts were imbedded deep in the ship's timbers. He almost gave way to despair, then slowly regained his composure. "We'll get someone down here soon," he promised Barnum. "When we do I'll fix that arm in shipshape fashion."

"I remember now, Mr. Murdock," said the sailor. "One o' them pirates drilled my arm with a pistol ball." He looked down. "There's blood all over, but I ain't bleedin' no more."

"You'll be all right then," said Jim, with a great deal more optimism than he felt. He looked up at the thin shafts of light coming through the grating. It was daylight, but whether morning or afternoon he had no way of telling. The heat was stifling enough 'tween decks to be high noon. He felt the perspiration form and run down his back. Practically no ventilation came through the opening; even breathing was difficult. For the first time he realized how thirsty he was. He ran his tongue over his parched and cracked lips. The gurgle of bilge water made him think of a bubbling brook. He shook his head. Better snap out of it, he cautioned himself; it might be a long time before Cruet let them have any food or water. He looked at the pathetic figures of his two sailors. Suddenly he realized Hardy was missing. He couldn't remember seeing him on the deck the night before after the pirates took over.

"Hews," he called. "What happened to Hardy?"

"I don't know, sir, unless they threw him over the side, too. Last time I saw him he was still steerin' the ship. 'Bout that time someone struck me with a belayin' pin and I don't remember anything after that."

"How about you, Barnum? Did you see Hardy?"

"I didn't see nothin', sir. They musta hit me first," Barnum answered. "I reckon I got hit and shot about the same time."

Jim thought for a minute. "Then neither of you saw Cruet fire into the *Victory?*"

"Fire into the *Victory!*" exclaimed Hews. "Was there a fight?" he asked in astonishment.

Jim quickly related the events of the night.

"And you say Captain Mellon thought it was us firin' into the ship?" Hews asked when Jim had finished.

"I guess he did," said Jim glumly.

"But couldn't he see you were bound and gagged, sir?"

"I doubt it," answered Jim reflectively. "It was pretty dark and I suspect the captain was too shocked by the *Rover's* broadside to think much at all."

For a moment there was silence in the hold. Jim knew what a bad spot he was in. If none of them got back to explain what had happened, he would be branded throughout the Navy as a deserter, mutineer, or worse. Some of his friends wouldn't believe the charge, but with Captain Mellon's condemnation of his conduct the official view would be black indeed.

The three men sat quietly, each with his own thoughts. Jim glanced at the grating from time to time, but it seemed forever before he noticed daylight waning. Almost with this discovery, he heard renewed activity on deck and a noise at the opening. He saw the grating move and heard it fall onto the deck with a loud thump. Cruet's swarthy face appeared at the coaming edge. He stared down into the hold.

"Hey, down there. How you fin' the beeg black hole?" he taunted.

"Send us down some water, Cruet," Jim demanded, "and give us something to eat."

The pirate captain chuckled evilly. "Ah! So the veree fine naval officaire ees thirsty, no? An' has much hungaire, too, eh?"

"You have to feed us, Cruet. We're prisoners of war."

Cruet roared with laughter. "Een truth, my fran',
you are a prisonaire. The question ees, do we feed you,
or do we feed the sharks?"

Jim heard a chorus of rough laughter follow the captain's cruel jest. He determined not to lose his temper
though.

"Cruet," he called. "One of my men is badly wounded.
Let me tend him."

"Ah. Ees too bad. I am so sorree," the captain mocked.
"I tell you thees. I, Antoine Cruet, weel tend your man.
I am a veree good doctaire. We throw heem ovaire the
side of the sheep, and voilà! you 'ave no more worree."

Jim heard another roar of laughter on deck. Moments
later he heard Cruet bark a quick order and saw a ladder
thrust into the hold. The opening darkened when a crew
member climbed through the hatch. A second pirate
followed the first. Each held a lantern in one hand and
a pistol in the other.

Jim shot a quick look at Barnum, whose drawn face
was bathed in sweat. Obviously the man was in great
pain. Poor Barnum probably wondered if the pirates
would actually throw him overboard, Jim thought, and
realized the renegade Frenchman was quite capable of
carrying out his threat.

The two pirates eyed the three Americans warily.
While one threatened Jim with his pistol, the other reached
down and unlocked the chain. Taking no chances, they
both then backed away and motioned to the ladder.

Jim rubbed his chafed wrists and flexed his aching
muscles. Lightheaded after his ordeal, he staggered to
the ladder and grabbed the rungs to steady himself. He
nodded toward the two American sailors. "Are you
going to let them topside, too?" he asked.

The two men only glared and motioned him up the ladder.

"I'll get some food and water for us," he promised Hews and Barnum. He turned and climbed painfully to the deck.

Jim found himself the object of considerable attention when he stood before the captain. Cruet was taking no chances; at least twenty of his cutthroats stood with him as he faced the young officer.

"Cruet, give my men water and food," demanded Jim.

"But, of course, Meestaire Murdock. Why for you theenk I breeng you on deck?" He motioned to the ladder. "Your fran's coming up, too."

Jim turned and saw Hews' head above the hatch coaming. Without a word to Cruet, he walked to the hatch and helped the man on deck. Since none of the pirates made a move to stop him, he waited until Barnum's anguished face appeared and helped him, too.

The exertion of the climb, short as it was, left the wounded man exhausted. Jim supported him and faced the sneering captain.

"This man is badly hurt, Cruet. Have one of your men bring me some hot water so I can tend his wound." Without waiting to see if his captor would comply, he helped Barnum remove his bloodstained shirt.

Jim quickly saw that the pistol ball had passed completely through the sailor's upper arm. Fortunately the shirt had matted with blood to staunch the flow and save Barnum's life. Jim pressed gently around the wound and along the bone. To his relief he discovered the bone intact. Barnum was in for serious trouble, however, if the wound wasn't cared for immediately. The midshipman had seen too many wounds fester and turn gangrenous in the tropics to make light of it. If he was to save

the arm, he must take care of it without delay. He turned
impatiently to the pirate captain.

"This man needs medical attention as you can well
see."

Cruet swaggered across the deck and glanced contemptuously at the wound.

"Ees no good, that arm. Eet weel nevaire get well
een thees climate." He turned to a huge black in the
group. "Pierre," he called. "We 'ave work for your
machete. We cut off the américain's arm. We save hees
life, eh?" He roared at his own joke.

The black laughed, his white teeth a bright slash
across his glistening black face. He dropped a hand to
the handle of a broad-bladed machete in his belt. The
other pirates crowded around to get a close view of their
shipmate's crude surgery.

"Mr. Murdock! Oh, no, sir! Don't let 'em cut off my
arm! Please, sir!" Barnum screamed, his chalk-white
face bathed in sweat.

Jim stepped between the black and the terrified sailor.
"Amputation is not necessary, Cruet," Jim said firmly.
"With proper care that arm will mend nicely."

Cruet shrugged. "Veree well. Me, I would t'row
heem ovaire the side. He die een two—t'ree days anyway."

"Nonsense!" exclaimed Jim. "Do I get the hot
water?"

Cruet studied the young midshipman's face for a moment; then turned to one of his men and growled a command. The man slipped away from the group on deck
and ran forward. Minutes later, he returned with a
bucket of hot water from the galley.

Jim in the meantime took off his shirt and ripped it
into strips. He folded several of these into small compresses. When the pirate dropped the bucket on deck,

the young officer held the wads of cloth in the steaming water. With great care he then wiped the blood away and cleaned the wound as best he could. He placed two other crudely sterilized compresses over the ugly opening and bound them in place with other strips. When finished, he looked his handiwork over and uttered a silent prayer that Barnum's robust health would do the rest.

"Better'n any sawbones coulda done, Mr. Murdock," said Barnum gratefully.

"It'll have to do for now," Jim replied. "When we get ashore, we'll get some proper medicine for it." He stood up and faced the watching pirate captain. "Now we'd like some food and water, Cruet," he demanded in a level voice.

The captain arched his eyebrows. "You 'ave not eaten?" he asked in mock surprise. "Ees bad 'ospitality, no? I, Antoine Cruet, weel feex." He turned to a crew member and rattled off an order. As the man started for the galley, Cruet caught him by the arm and whispered in his ear. He turned a smiling face on the American. "We geeve you the best we 'ave, mon ami." With a wide sweep of his arm he motioned to the deck. "Please be seat. Eet weel soon be 'ere."

Jim nodded to the two sailors to indicate they were to be seated, then sat down himself. He wasn't sure Cruet meant what he said, but was glad to sit down anyway. He slid alongside Barnum to give the still-fearful sailor courage.

Moments later the circle of pirates opened up. A man carrying three bowls stepped toward the Americans. Jim's heart gave a leap when he saw they were finally going to get food. As the man walked closer his elation turned to amazement.

"Hardy!" he shouted. "Thank God you're all right."

Jim jumped to his feet. "We were afraid they'd got you, man!"

Hardy's face showed no expression as he handed a bowl to each of his shipmates.

Jim placed his bowl on deck and started to help Barnum with his. "We're sure glad to have you back with us, Hardy," Jim exclaimed as he started to spoon for the almost helpless Barnum. "You reckon you could get us some water, now?" He looked up at the helmsman.

Cruet moved up beside Hardy and put his arm around the seaman's shoulders.

"I theenk the so-smart young officaire make beeg meestake, eh, mon ami?" He leered at Hardy.

Jim almost dropped his bowl. He stared unbelievingly at his former shipmate.

"Hardy! You can't mean—"

"Tell heem, mon ami," Cruet urged. "Tell heem you now fight for Capitaine Cruet, your veree good fran', ees eet not?"

The pirates broke into loud guffaws as the midshipman showed his amazement.

"Why you dirty—" Hews spat the words.

"Hardy! You can't mean you've joined this band of cutthroats? Man, you don't know what you're doing!" cried Jim.

Hardy slowly turned his back on the midshipman.

Cruet pointed to the ugly red welts crisscrossing the seaman's back.

"You wheep heem right eento my crew," he gloated. "Now maybe you not so smart, eh, Meestaire Murdock?"

★

CHAPTER 5

Pirates' Lair

THE PIRATE stronghold on Gonave was a scene of incredible disorder. As the small boat carrying Jim and his two men moved through the glassy waters of the small bay, Jim could see the beach littered with boats and barges, none properly secured, and all untended. Here and there a larger barge, too heavy to drag out of the water, slanted against the sand, with bilges obviously full of water. A dozen huts, for the most part constructed of odd wreckage, lined the flat ground behind the beach. Beyond these the mountains of the rugged island loomed dark green in the early morning light, their sides covered with heavy foliage. A blazing fire crackled in the area before the huts, its light revealing that most, if not all, of the pirates preferred the open for sleeping.

With a shout, one of the pirates near the fire awakened his closest companions. Their combined shouting in turn roused the whole camp. Hurrying down to the water's edge, they waited for the boat to land.

Jim glanced at Cruet in the stern. A smile crossed the captain's evil face as he watched the camp swarm to the sand. His pride in capturing a fine big brig like the *Rover* was written all over his face.

The prisoners felt the boat grind into sand a few feet from the beach. Cruet ordered them to wade in and followed with a lordly swagger.

The pirates stared briefly at the Americans but for the most part they seemed anxious to congratulate their leader.

Taking advantage of their preoccupation for the moment, Jim used the opportunity to look them over carefully. Never had he seen a more desperate group of ruffians. All were dressed in the castoff finery of victims of their many raids. One even sported a shirt of heavy brocade, obviously a part of a lady's dress. In only one respect were they uniform: each carried a long knife or machete in his belt. Several, in addition, carried muskets, holding on to them as if they feared their shipmates might steal them. The whites, virtually indistinguishable from their more swarthy fellows by reason of their dirty skin, welcomed the captain with even more enthusiasm than the others.

"This is a rare gang o' cutthroats, Mr. Murdock," Hews murmured.

"Aye," agreed Jim in a whisper. "Show no fear though, or they'll torture us unmercifully." He moved closer to Barnum. "How's the arm feeling?"

"Throbbin' a mite, but I reckon I can expect that," the seaman answered.

"I'll have a look at it, first chance I get." Jim glanced at the pirates crowded around the captain. "Careful, now. Here comes Cruet," he warned, as he saw the group part to let their leader through.

Cruet strutted up to the three prisoners and looked them over with a leer. "Now, Meestaire Murdock, we decide what to do weeth you. We take a vote lak true républicains." He swung around and faced his men, raised his hands for quiet and launched into a rapid explanation of the capture. Jim saw the cutthroats grin fiendishly. At the end of Cruet's boastful speech they yelled and waved their machetes in the air.

The pirate leader turned to the Americans again. He shrugged and spread his hands expressively. "I, Antoine Cruet, 'ave done what I can, but my children desire your death. I am veree sorree, my fran's."

"Nonsense, Cruet," Jim said. "I don't care what this bunch of renegades wants. You kill three Navy men in cold blood and the commodore will wipe this place out if he has to use the whole squadron." He watched the captain's smile fade. Hurrying on he continued, "Furthermore, Rigaud won't look with favor on the murder of hostages. We've got a few of his officers prisoner, you know, and he'll never get them back except in an exchange."

Cruet frowned. Obviously it had never occurred to him that General Rigaud would be interested in the Americans. He had thought only of catering to the animal savagery of his followers.

Jim went on. "Suppose Rigaud does take all of Hispaniola and set himself up as ruler. Do you think the United States will ever recognize a country that murders helpless captives? If you haven't thought of this, you'd better. I'm sure Rigaud has, and you'd better be prepared to answer a lot of questions if you kill us."

The midshipman could see he had Cruet turning over the matter in his shrewd mind. If only I've convinced him, thought Jim. Even a short delay in carrying out the will of the pirates might give the Americans a chance to escape.

Cruet stared for a long minute at the young officer, then turned slowly, a placating smile on his face, to address his band again.

"Mes enfants!" he yelled, to get their attention again, then launched into another long talk.

Jim watched smiles of anticipation give way to scowls when it dawned on the pirates they were to miss some fun. He heard Cruet mention General Rigaud several times and the necessity of having their commander in chief take final action on the prisoners.

Several of the band started to raise their voices in protest. It was quite apparent that Cruet's hold over his followers was but slight. He saw the captain grow taut, the amiability of his manner disappear.

One huge pirate, bolder than the rest, stepped forward, his machete held aloft for attention. "Non! Non!" he yelled.

Cruet directed all his attention to this threat to his leadership. Speaking rapidly, he tried to calm the man down. Evidently he could make no headway, for the man waved his machete wildly and continued to shout. Finally Cruet drew a pistol from his belt and threatened the protesting pirate. At this move, the big fellow seemed to lose his head completely. He took a step forward, menacing his leader with the bright blade. Cruet's knuckles whitened on the pistol grip. A sharp "crack" followed and the entire group froze into silence.

The burly pirate stood stockstill for a few seconds, a look of complete astonishment on his face. He bent his head and stared stupidly at the widening circle of blood on his shirt front. He touched the spot with his fingers in amazement. He began to sway on his feet. A moment later he dropped to the sand.

The remainder of the pirates stared at the lifeless figure then back at Cruet. There was a muttering of curses, but as the pirates were leaderless now in their re-

volt, their low-voiced protests died down. Slowly the
gathering broke up, as by ones and twos they withdrew
to other parts of the compound. No one cared to test
his strength against their captain. Callous for the most
part to sudden death, they seemed to forget the incident
the minute the crowd dissolved. Cruet, confident once
again, called to two of them, motioned to the body and
gave quiet orders.

With much grunting and cursing, the pirates dragged
their dead compatriot over to the water's edge. They
toppled the body into a small pirogue, got in themselves
and commenced to paddle. When well off the beach
they unceremoniously rolled the body into the water.

Jim watched, horrified, as the corpse rose once then
disappeared in a welter of boiling water; a school of
deadly barracuda had found a victim.

Cruet turned to Jim and thumped his chest. "You see,
I, Antoine Cruet, am boss, is it not so?"

"You're a cold-blooded murderer, Cruet," said Jim.
"But perhaps we owe you our lives. However," he continued, "in saving us you've saved your own neck, so I
guess that evens the score."

For the moment he had Cruet believing he must keep
the prisoners alive. He wanted to keep it that way.

"Now I suggest you get me some medicine so I can
take care of Barnum's arm. Otherwise you'll only have
two hostages to tell General Rigaud about."

Cruet scowled. "We 'ave no medicines!"

"Then get me a pan to boil some water in and some
decent rags to bind the wound."

Cruet glanced at Barnum, thought for a moment, then
turned and ordered one of his men to bring the needed
supplies. When the ragged fellow ran off, Cruet swung
again on Jim. "You weel stay een that hut." He pointed

to a crude shack nearby. "Eef you try the escape, I keel
you. Comprenez? Even mon général cannot protest eef
you are keel during the escape."

Jim turned his back on the pirate and started for the
hut, calling over his shoulder for the two sailors to follow
him. He looked the temporary prison over carefully as he
neared it. As a prison it was a farce, hung together as it
was by ropes and worm-eaten boards. Insecure as it
might be, he knew the pirates would guard it well. An
escape would have to be plotted with care. With this
thought in mind, he carefully studied the surrounding
area.

The hut rested on palmetto logs, placing the floor
some two feet above the sand. Although the front faced
the open compound, there were but a few yards separating
the rear of the small building and the heavy growth of
tropic vegetation surrounding the compound. There at
least was an avenue of escape! Jim quickly noted the
position of the two nearest huts and saw that they were
rather far removed. He had little time to see more before
Cruet ordered the three prisoners into the hut.

Jim turned at the door.

"When will I get the rags and pan to fix Barnum's
wound?" he asked.

Cruet shrugged. "Get een the hut. You weel be
told when eet ees ready," he growled.

Strangely enough the pirate did not close the sagging
door. He motioned to two of his men. They took up a
guard position by the door. Each carried a machete in
his hand and a pistol in his belt. That they had no love
for their job was obvious from the dark looks they threw
at the open door. Jim figured they'd like nothing better
than to have the Americans try an escape.

It was a full two hours later before a dirty and un-

kempt pirate appeared with a battered pan and a handful
of evil-smelling rags. Jim took them with distaste. If
Cruet had deliberately tried to infect Barnum's wound,
he could have accomplished his purpose in no better way.
The midshipman glanced at the remains of his white
stockings. They would have to serve. He'd boil them
half an hour; that would sterilize them, or at least boil
most of the dirt out. As to what he would use to clean
the wound, he didn't know. He'd seen ordinary wounds
cleaned with water, then sprinkled with gunpowder. He
wasn't convinced of the efficacy of this cure, because as
many men seemed to die as to recover. He knew also
that in the mountains of Virginia the settlers poured corn
whisky over wounds. Rum—and this seemed to be ample
in the camp—might help, but he doubted if the pirates
would part with any. At any cost he must however get
some water from the guards and find a way to boil it.

Jim didn't know what orders the two pirates had been
given, but he determined to get Barnum's arm fixed. He
picked up the pan and walked to the door. "Water," he
said and pointed to the empty pan.

The swarthy guard exchanged looks with his companion and shrugged. Both then turned their backs on
the hut. One moved to a nearby palm tree and sat down
in the shade.

Jim hesitated for a moment, reached down and un-
clasped the silver buckle from one of his shoes. He
stepped up to the guard remaining at the door and placed
it in his hand. "Water," he repeated.

The guard turned the buckle over in his hand, ex-
amining it closely. With the point of his machete blade
he drew a scratch across the bright surface. Satisfied the
buckle was of real silver, he shot a furtive look around

the compound and turned to Jim. He drew the pistol
from his belt, cocked it, and pointed toward the jungle.

Jim walked to the edge of the compound and saw a
well-defined path leading inland. He could hear the
heavy breathing of his guard close behind him as he
stepped into the thick jungle of cabbage palms, gris-gris
trees and undergrowth. Not twenty-five yards in, he suddenly broke into a tiny glade, banked on all sides with
deep green ferns. Running through the glade, a small
stream trickled cold and clear to one end where a small,
crystal pool lay smooth and undisturbed. To the hot,
tired midshipman it was a vision of heaven. Without a
backward glance at his guard he ran forward and dropped
to his knees to drink deeply of its cold waters.

The lonely glade, only a stone's throw from the pirate
camp, was a world unto itself. Jim watched swarms of
warblers and thrushes, startled by his sudden movement,
beat the air with their wings and head for the treetops.
He marked the progress of a covey of quail as the alarmed
birds scurried through the ferns, shaking the broad but
fragile leaves. In a tall icaco tree further inland, a group
of brilliant green and yellow parrots screamed in protest
at the trespassing humans in the glade. What a beautiful
spot, thought Jim.

The beauty of the space made no impression on Jim's
guard. He pointed to the pan and made a threatening
motion with his pistol. Jim reluctantly filled the iron
vessel, stood up and headed back toward the hut.

Barnum and Hews drank greedily of the water; Barnum in particular seemed unable to get his fill. Jim
laid the flat of his hand on the quartermaster's forehead.
The man was burning up with fever! Without any comment he led him to the door and across the compound to

the fire. He saw one of the guards follow them but paid
no attention to his presence. Raking a few coals from the
larger fire, he then built up a support with some loose
coral heads and set the pan over the fire. Satisfied the
water would boil in a few minutes, he seated Barnum
nearby.

"How's it feel?" he asked.

Barnum shook his head slowly. "Reckon it ain't
gettin' much better, sir. She's swole up more'n ever."

"Let me take a look," said Jim.

The midshipman unwrapped the stained bandages
and exposed the wound. Although clear of dirt it presented an ugly red picture. Quickly he examined the
arm in all directions for the telltale streaks of further infection. Seeing none, he breathed a sigh of relief and
began preparations for a new dressing.

Jim allowed the water to boil for a long time. The
stockings appeared clean when he finally fished them out
of the pan. He gave them a chance to cool then began
bandaging.

"Mr. Murdock," said Barnum in a low voice, "did ye
see that pirogue farthest up the beach?"

"Aye," muttered Jim. "A fast boat if I ever saw one."

"Big enough to sail and small enough to paddle,"
whispered the quartermaster. "Easy to get into the water,
too!"

"Could be," answered Jim quietly. "We'll keep our
eye on it." He stood up and said loudly, "That'll hold
for a while, Barnum," as if only the injured man was on
his mind.

As he helped Barnum to his feet, Jim wondered
whether the makeshift treatment would be of any help.
While the wound showed no infection as yet, he wished
mightily that he had proper medicine for the man. With-

out it, Barnum might take a turn for the worse, and quickly, too. He let his eyes wander around the camp as he helped the quartermaster along toward their prison, mentally fixing the location of every hut. He stole another glance at the pirogue, so temptingly near their own hut. Suddenly he knew what they must do. And they must do it that night!

★

CHAPTER 6

Foiled!

SHORTLY before dark, the three Americans watched the pirates gather in the compound for the evening meal: the only meal they had seen their captors actually prepare. They had watched their guards eat fruit, from time to time, but nothing that had been cooked. Coconuts were plentiful, as was the plumlike fruit of the caremita tree, which required no more energy than the plucking of it.

For the evening meal, the pirates made elaborate preparations. Great fires were built to provide thick beds of hot coals, and latticelike racks of green wood were fashioned and laid across the coals. From somewhere deep in the inland savannah, pirates dragged in the carcasses of wild cattle. These they skinned and gutted, then cut the lean, red meat in long strips, which in turn were stretched across the green wood-racks. Great bunches of plantains, a red-brown fruit, were baked in the hot coals. Cabbage palms simmered in a greasy liquid on smaller fires. Jim eyed the food hungrily. A decent share would do much to restore the strength and spirits of his men.

After darkness had fallen, and the pirates had gorged themselves on food washed down with an abundance of fiery rum and milder palm wine, someone thought to bring rations to the prisoners. They ate well but with some restraint, Jim having cautioned his men to save some of the tough strips of meat.

"D'ye think we actually have a chance to get clear, Mr. Murdock?" asked Hews.

Jim glanced through the open door. "If they keep eating and swilling rum, I'm sure we have," he answered. "No man can stow vittles away like that and not fall into a stupor."

As if to prove his words, the three Americans watched two new guards stagger up to the hut to relieve their compatriots on duty. Both were dull-eyed with over-eating and drinking.

"And if we do get clear of the island? What then?" asked Barnum.

"It can't be more'n forty miles to Port-au-Prince," answered Jim. "With any breeze at all, we could make it there in the pirogue, by dawn. We could hug the coast for a while; we'd be harder to see that way. Perhaps we might even pick up one of the squadron cruising in the channel. The *Victory* herself might well have turned back toward Port-au-Prince."

Hews cleared his throat. "Mr. Murdock, I don't want to sound like an old woman . . . but if the *Victory* took a lot of damage . . . then maybe she didn't go nowhere."

Jim shook his head slowly. "I doubt that, Hews. She did take a surprise broadside, but my guess is that Rigaud's ship cleared out, rather than stand up to a Navy ship. Then, too, I didn't see much damage to the *Rover,* so you can be certain Cruet didn't help his friend in the *Tres Amis* much."

"I hope you're right, sir."

"I feel confident of it. Now let's go over the plans we discussed this afternoon." Jim motioned them toward the rear of the hut. "We'll wait another hour; then I'll go out through the back." He reached down and tested the panel, the lower lashings of which he'd cut earlier in the afternoon. "I'll pick up a half-dozen coconuts— the ground's full of them in the glade—and fill the pan with water. When I get back, we'll wait until the guards are either dozing or busy then make a dash for it. Once clear of land, we can hoist the sail. Do you both understand?"

Each of the two men agreed that he did.

Hews walked to the open door, looked out and then beckoned to Jim. "Mr. Murdock," he whispered excitedly, "those two men are asleep already."

Jim ran lightly to the door. "This is better than I'd hoped for!" he exclaimed. "Now we can get away sooner than we'd planned." He darted a look toward the pirogue. It was still there, although in the darkness it showed no more than a black spot on the lighter beach. Looking back to the campfires, he noted with satisfaction that but few glowing coals remained. They cast little or no light beyond the immediate circle of the fires.

Hews laid a restraining hand on Jim's shoulder. "Mr. Murdock, I don't like it," he said, in a troubled voice.

"You don't like what?"

"I don't like the whole pattern. Somehow, it looks too easy. First, they put us in this hut and don't even shut the door. Then they leave a tidy little craft almost in our laps, so to speak. To top that off, the guards go right to sleep." He shook his head slowly. "I don't like it at all. I keep thinkin' how Cruet licked his chops when he said he'd kill us if we tried to escape."

Jim moved uneasily. Hews had voiced his own fears. What the man said was true. He knew it and couldn't shake the thought from his own mind. Yet why would Cruet make such elaborate plans just to kill them? Jim

honestly believed the pirate wanted to turn them over
to General Rigaud and take credit for their capture.

"And ye notice too, sir, that Cruet ain't around
checkin' up on us," said Hews. "He ain't been around
any since mornin'. It ain't like the sharp rogue to be so
unseamanlike."

"Perhaps," said Jim. "On the other hand, this may
be just their careless way of doing things." He stood
silently for a minute, watching the sleeping figures of the
guards. "At least, this way," he continued, "we have a
fighting chance. It's a chance we'll have to take!"

"Aye, sir," agreed Hews, reluctantly. "We're with
you."

Although Jim knew that any delay wasted precious
minutes of darkness, he forced himself to wait until there
was absolutely no sight or sound of activity in the camp.
It must have been close to midnight before he cautiously
raised the loosened panel and eased his sturdy body
through the back wall. He wrapped the pan in his
jacket to eliminate any possibility of noise in case he fell
or ran into a tree.

The path that seemed so clear and well-defined in
broad daylight was a tortuous nightmare to follow in the
blackness of the jungle. By feel and sense, he moved
forward, step by cautious step. Once, when his foot
disturbed the nocturnal wanderings of a small rodent,
he almost dropped the pan in alarm. Again, his passage
wakened a group of sleeping birds. The noise of their
flight seemed loud enough to wake the dead! He stood
motionless for a full two minutes to listen for sounds from
the camp. Hearing none, he pushed on to the glade.

He had no difficulty locating coconuts; he could hardly
avoid stepping on them. Again he filled the pan and
headed back toward the hut. The return trip he found

much easier, requiring only a few minutes to reach the hut.

"Ain't been a sound out of the camp," said Barnum excitedly. "Them guards didn't stir once."

"Most likely the whole camp's drunk," Hews put in. "I feel better about things now, sir. If you can get to the stream and back, I reckon we can make it to the boat."

"How about you, Barnum?" said Jim. "You feel well enough to make the attempt?"

"Yes, sir," whispered the sailor, urgently. "All I want to do is get outa this place. Every time I close my eyes I see that big fellow with the machete."

Jim moved to the door and took a careful look around the compound. He wished he could shake his persistent uneasiness. The camp was silent; his men had seen no movement while he was away. Everything seemed perfect. Perhaps he was too cautious. He turned to face the two sailors.

"Now for it, boys. Follow me. I'll hug the edge of the clearing until we reach the shadows of those cabbage palms." He drew them to the door and pointed to a blot of black on the edge of the clearing near the beach. "If we get that far safely, we'll wait a few minutes and move on to the boat." He took a deep breath. "Let's go, men," he said, calmly. "Hews, count to ten slowly after I duck out the panel; then follow me."

Jim slipped out the back of the hut, holding the pan of water carefully. He wished mightily he could get rid of it, but knew what a boat trip under the hot sun could be without water. Then, too, if they had to hide on land, he would always have something to boil water in for Barnum's wound.

He moved forward a few steps, hesitated, then started

forward again. Behind him he heard a slight squeak, as Hews raised the panel to leave the hut.

Suddenly a body launched itself from the undergrowth to knock him flat. The pan flew out of his hands to land with a clatter on a few loose coral rocks. He heard his assailant scream at the top of his voice:

"Ho! The camp! Ho!"

Jim recognized Hardy's voice. He twisted savagely in the man's grip, trying desperately to drive his fist in the man's face.

"Hardy, you bilge rat!" he cried, through clenched teeth. "I'll kill you for this!"

"Quiet!" growled Hardy. He held the point of his knife at the downed midshipman's chest. "Move, and I'll drive six inches of steel into your ribs," he said in a loud voice.

Within seconds, the whole camp burst into life. Campfires blazed high, as several pirates threw tinder-dry palm fronds onto the glowing coals.

Holding Jim at knife point, Hardy yanked him to his feet and swung him around to face the camp. Jim darted a quick look at the rear of his hut and saw with relief that Hews and Barnum had stayed there as planned if he did run into trouble. He braced himself to face alone what punishment they might give him.

Out of the corner of his eye, he caught a movement near the pirogue and to his amazement watched a group of pirates emerge from the cluster of cabbage palms nearby. As they closed in on him, he saw they were all armed with naked machetes and led by Antoine Cruet. It suddenly dawned on him that if they had reached the clump of palms, they would have been waylaid by Cruet's picked gang. He relaxed in Hardy's grip and muttered over his shoulder, "Maybe I owe you an apology, Hardy."

"Shut up!" shouted Hardy, and sent the officer stumbling toward the pirate captain with a push.

Hardy stalked after him, his face contorted with rage. "I caught him sneakin' out after water," he shouted at Cruet. "I thought you were going to keep 'em under guard." He pointed to the empty pan on the sand. "They want water, let 'em beg for it," he growled. "For all o' me they can die of thirst!" He favored the midshipman with a look of pure hatred.

Cruet turned cold eyes on Jim, studied his face for a long minute as if trying to reach a decision. He glanced at the pan, then shifted his cunning eyes to Hardy.

"I was—" started Jim.

Whack! Hardy reached out and clouted the midshipman on the side of the head. "Speak when yer spoken to!" he ripped out, savagely.

Cruet held up his hand. "Ees enough, mon ami," he cautioned and swung his eyes back to Jim. "You 'ave been veree fortunate, américain," he said. "Our zealous, or I should say, overzealous, Hardy 'ave save you much trouble." He swung on Hardy again with a smile. "I theenk we have discovaire the best guard for these prisonaires. Take them to the hut, fran' Hardy."

Hardy walked up to the midshipman.

"You heard the man! March!" he snarled.

Jim stared at his former shipmate coldly; then turned and walked across the compound. Was Hardy putting on an act? Did he mean to save the three Americans from Cruet's assassins? Or was he really trying to raise his position with Cruet by preventing a possible escape? You would think the man would give some small sign if he intended to protect his former shipmates. Why hadn't he come to the rear of the hut in the darkness and explained the trap to Jim? The midshipman shook his head. He couldn't understand it.

"Mr. Murdock! Sir! What happened?" Hews cried. "We heard all the yelling, and when we looked out the doorway, the guards were standing there ready for us."

Jim related the story of his encounter with Hardy.

"Let me get my hands on that scum! He'll get worse than the cat if I do!" Hews growled.

"Steady, man," counseled Jim. He told the two seamen of Cruet's party.

"You mean then that Hardy actually saved our lives?" asked Barnum.

"I don't know," answered Jim, shaking his head. "Maybe he did mean to, and maybe he didn't." He rubbed the side of his head. "If he's acting he's putting on a convincing act!"

"What do we do now, Mr. Murdock?" Hews asked. "They'll be watchin' us closer'n ever now."

"I don't think there's much we can do now," said Jim, disgustedly. "We just wait now and see what happens. There is a chance that Cruet will deliver us to General Rigaud without any further delay."

"Ain't that quite a trip, sir?" asked Barnum.

"Aye," said Jim. "We'd have to cross over to the mainland, a good twenty-mile trip, and then it's at least forty miles over the mountains to Jacmel."

"That's quite a walk," muttered Barnum.

Jim felt sudden compassion for the wounded man. "We'll make it, Barnum," he promised, reassuringly. "Keep up your courage."

★

CHAPTER 7

Friend or Enemy?

CRUET was smart, thought Jim, not to risk his newly won brig on this trip to the mainland. With it safe inside the small bay, the pirate could approach his general with a record of achievement. The three small sailing pirogues they were now in would be no loss at all if they were captured. They had left the island of Gonave at night, however, to avoid contact with any men-of-war in the channel. Cruet wanted to keep his prisoners, too.

Jim glanced ruefully at his manacled hands. He eyed the heavy stone tied to the manacles with a wry smile. Easy enough to dump him over the side and leave no evidence, if they were sighted by an American ship. The pirates looked not unlike the island fishermen, except for the weapons they carried. Cruet was shrewd all right. He took no chances.

The midshipman straightened out his cramped legs as far as the confines of the narrow boat would permit and wished mightily they'd soon get to land. He studied the mountainous coastline up ahead. Strange, how such a beautiful island could harbor so much savagery and terror. From the sheer headland on his left to the rugged mountains on his right, towering blue and purple in the pre-dawn sky, the wide panorama was a breathtaking view of the Jewel of the West Indies. Hispaniola: the land

Columbus grew to love more than any other. Dazzling white sand beaches capped the heads of the many tiny coves holding back the incredibly lush, tropical verdure of palm and fern that grew almost to the water. Behind and above the coastal palm groves, tangled masses of thorny acacia climbed the sheer slopes of the mountains. Even so far at sea, Jim could recognize the scent of jasmine and the more delicate odors of orange blossoms and cassia. It could almost set a man dreaming of paradise, to close one's eyes.

A sudden rocking of the boat jarred Jim out of his dreams. Cruet was hoisting the wide lateen sail. A bright red streak on the eastern horizon prefaced dawn, and the pirate intended to catch the first whiff of morning breeze. The other two pirogues quickly followed the motion and very shortly began to glide effortlessly across the smooth sea, as the breeze picked up.

Not one of the ten pirates with Cruet had spoken, except when necessary, during the night's trip. For the most part they dozed, or when their turn came, paddled listlessly. Jim was convinced that none of them relished the trip to Jacmel. A forty-mile hike across the mountains was not their idea of good living. He noticed that Cruet never slept; doubtless he did not trust his men too far. He paid a pretty price in eternal vigilance to be leader of this band of cutthroats, thought Jim. Not one of them looked as if he would trust his own mother.

Now that the sails carried the craft along, the men lost some of their surliness. Cruet was definitely headed for a cove distinguished only by the depth of a ravine folded into the mountains behind the beach. This ravine must shelter a trail through the mountains, Jim figured.

Thirty minutes later, the three boats were close enough for Jim to see long low swells breaking in a smother of feathering spray over a protecting reef. For the life of him, he could see no break in the coral that they could use as a passage; yet just before they entered the welter of brilliant spray, the leading pirogue abruptly changed its course. It slid easily through a narrow channel into a sheltered lagoon. He grudgingly gave his captors credit; they knew how to handle a small boat. No wonder the American Navy had so much trouble running them down.

The boat grounded on the sand beach, and Jim turned to see Cruet bow with mock politeness.

"And now, m'sieu Murdock. Please to step ashore. From here to Jacmel ees a long trip." He called to the other pirogues. "Get those cursed américains ashore!"

Jim stood helplessly on the beach, holding the heavy stone in his hands, and watched a pirate push the suffering Barnum into the shallow water. He saw Hardy, a member of that same boat crew, ignore the brutal act and jump lightly to the sand beach. Barnum stood up in the knee-deep water, staggered to dry sand and sank exhausted to the beach.

Cruet moved up behind the midshipman and spoke in a low voice. "Ees forty mile to Jacmel, mon ami. That one weel fin' the trail veree bad. Eet ees better we dump heem een the bay, no?"

"Cruet, you're a cold-blooded monster."

The pirate shrugged. "Ees your affair then. Eef he does not keep up with the rest . . ." He made a slicing motion across his throat with his forefinger, chuckled evilly and turned away.

"Surely you're going to free our hands," Jim said.

"Per'aps," Cruet called back. "We see firs' 'ow you be'ave."

Whatever his intentions might have been ultimately, the pirate captain did not at once free their hands.

Barnum and Hews stood with their officer and watched the ragged band drag the pirogues into a tangle of underbrush far back on the beach. They carefully concealed the location with foliage. Cruet ordered the Americans off the sand beach, and his men swept it smooth with giant palm leaves. When they had finished, no trace of their landing remained. Satisfied with the job, Cruet joined the three Americans.

"Ees a long hard treep across the mountains," he said. "I free the 'ands so you do not 'old us up. But wan small move een the wrong direction and we keel, comprenez?"

"We understand, Cruet," said Jim. He looked over the band of menacing pirates. "There are only three of us, unarmed, against your ten. Are you afraid we'll overpower you?"

Cruet's face darkened in anger. "I do not mean, of a necessity, that you weel escape, mon ami." He shifted his sly eyes to Barnum, who was obviously having difficulty holding the heavy stone in his hands. "Ever' man mus' keep up," he added, meaningfully.

The pirate was right about one thing, thought Jim, after a taste of the rugged mountain trail: it was going to be a rough trip. Whether they were testing their prisoners' ability to keep up or were actually in a hurry, the pirates set a lively pace. Barnum struggled along manfully but without the combined efforts of both his companions would have fallen far behind in the first ten minutes. Jim knew the pirates would not hesitate to cut the seaman's throat and leave him behind for the buzzards and carrion crows soaring high above their heads. Barnum was not unaware of their presence, and the very sight of them gave him strength to carry on.

By the time the group stopped at noon, the trail had

carried them high into the mountains. From their vantage point on a ledge high on the sheer mountainside, Jim got a breathtaking view of the shoreline and sea far below. But with Barnum almost at the point of collapse, he had things other than scenery to worry about. Until they reached the narrow trail in the higher elevations, he and Hews had been able to support the wounded man. To walk three abreast now was impossible, and they must take turns supporting their companion.

All three captives dropped to the ground exhausted when Cruet called a halt. The pirates pulled food out of greasy bags slung over their shoulders and commenced to eat.

"Eat!" ordered the pirate captain and threw a chunk of red boucan, roasted meat, on the ground before them.

Jim retrieved the food, wiped the dirt off it and tore it into three pieces. He handed his companions each a piece, then set to work chewing on the tough but strangely flavorful meat.

Cruet ordered Hardy to take a coconut shell filled with water to the prisoners. He handed it to Jim without comment. When Hews glared at his former shipmate, Hardy turned his back and rejoined the pirates.

A few minutes later, and the party was underway again. By midafternoon Jim wondered how much longer they could keep up. For Barnum, feverish and weak, the effort was almost beyond human endurance. Both Jim and Hews were feeling the drain on their own strength in the hot sun. Even the higher altitudes did little to cool its pitiless rays.

Just when it seemed they could no longer endure more, the party came to a halt. Jim looked at the head of the line and saw Cruet staring down the mountain. He let Barnum sag to the ground and moved up behind the party of gesticulating pirates. They had passed the crest of the mountain and stood on a ledge overlooking a broad and fertile valley that stretched for miles in each direction.

Far to the left, Jim saw the object of their excited attention. Great mushrooms of billowing black smoke covered a wide area of the level green valley. From the orderliness of the fields in that direction, he assumed he saw canefields afire. He caught the word "Toussaint" in the pirates' excited jabbering. His eyes followed a pointing arm to see a body of troops strung out like ants along a dusty road far below.

Suddenly, the implication of what he saw struck him: Toussaint L'Ouverture's armies were in General Rigaud's territory. Burning and pillaging their way through the country, they were undoubtedly headed for Jacmel and a showdown with Rigaud's troops. His spirits soared. If only they could get to . . .

" 'Ave no hope for escape, m'sieu Murdock," Cruet said suddenly. "When Général Rigaud hear of thees eenvasion of his countree—pouf! He wipe them away like leetle bugs." Cruet swept his men with a smiling glance of confidence. "Ees not true, my cheeldren?"

Jim watched their uncertain smiles and saw that none shared their leader's confidence.

"We camp 'ere for the night, my fran's," Cruet said, with a quick look at the lowering sun. "We 'ave made good time, my braves. I, Antoine Cruet, am proud of you."

Jim eyed the crafty leader. Cruet was too jovial, too obviously confident. It was but a mask to hide his real concern, the midshipman was sure. Turning, he hastened back to his companions and explained the new development.

"Hang it, sir, if we could just get to 'em, Toussaint's

troops would give us protection," muttered Hews. He glanced furtively at the group of pirates. "D'ye think there's a chance o' breakin' away?"

From the moment Jim sighted the troops on the plain below, his mind had raced over a dozen schemes for getting down to them. Now as he watched Barnum, pitiful in his helplessness, he realized they could never make it down an unknown trail at night, even if they managed to escape. The gamble for three strong men would be

hazardous, but with Barnum in his present state, such a trip would be suicide. He glanced at the sailor again and saw that the wounded man was watching him steadily.

"Leave me behind, Mr. Murdock," he pleaded. "You and Hews can get away tonight and make it easy." He put a hand up to his swollen arm. "It ain't as if you're desertin' me, sir. I know I can't last much longer. Please, sir, you and Hews make a run for it."

"Nonsense, man," said Jim, gruffly. "You're talking

a lot of rubbish. You're going to be all right. When has
a little hole in the arm stopped an American sailor?" He
tried to put confidence in his voice. "Cruet will probably tie us up proper tonight, anyway. Just be patient
and don't give up. We'll get out of this together."

"Stow that gab, you rats."

The three Americans looked up to see Hardy standing
over them.

"Captain says fer you to move over there." He
pointed to a hollow space in the sheer rock wall back of
the ledge. "Now git!"

"Blast you, Hardy," growled Hews, his face twisted
in rage. He started to his feet, both fists clenched.

Hardy scooped up a heavy stick from the ground and
took a step forward. "Just try it," he threatened the
sailor loudly. "I'd like nothin' better'n to crack that
thick skull o' yours!"

"Don't strike that man, Hardy." Jim spoke in a level
commanding voice.

"Oh! So you'd like a taste, too, *Mister* Murdock,"
cried Hardy. He took a threatening step toward the
young midshipman. "Maybe you'd like a dozen o' *my*
cat," he jeered, shaking the stick in Jim's face.

"Hardy, my fran'. We mus' save them for the jour-
nee," called Cruet laughingly. "Your time weel come,"
he promised.

Jim and his two companions ignored the jibe and
walked to the hollow in the cliff. They sat down with
their backs to the rock. As they watched, the sun, a
blazing ball in the west, dropped below the distant mountains across the plain, leaving their peaks touched with
gold for a few minutes as if reluctant to abandon such a
beautiful land. Below them the broad valley dissolved

from deep purple into a black abyss, broken only by the glowing canefields in the distance and a tiny flicker of light here and there, indicating a plantation.

With darkness, the night air turned cold. Jim was surprised at the sudden drop in temperature, even though he knew they were high in the pine-tree belt of the upper elevations.

Cruet permitted a fire, well-shielded on the valley side. The three prisoners watched its pale light bathe the circle of pirates clustered around it and envied them the warmth.

Jim saw the pirate captain lean over toward Hardy and nod in the direction of the prisoners. Hardy picked up three pieces of rope and walked over to the three Americans.

He growled deep in his throat and jerked savagely on the ropes as he tied them securely. After he had finished, he examined each knot carefully. He favored them with a leer, spat on the ground at their feet and then turned and swaggered back to the fire.

If Jim thought Cruet would relax his vigilance, in view of the fact that he and his companions were well-tied, he was in error. The pirate had no intention of leaving the Americans unguarded. Jim watched the ragged band draw lots. One dark brute, his face hideously scarred with old knife cuts, cursed when he found he was first, left the group around the fire and stalked toward the prisoners. He looked over their bonds with a critical eye, then took a seat on the ground in front of them.

Jim, his body throbbing with fatigue and pain, closed his eyes, but sleep wouldn't come. He turned over plan after plan in his mind and discarded each as impractical. His deep concern for Barnum and the man's desperate need for medical attention occupied all his thoughts. He racked his brain to recall some native herb that might have value, but his knowledge of such matters was indeed scant. He made a silent vow that no matter what part of the world he might be stationed in if he escaped this time, the first learning he would seek of the land would be native cures.

Sleep finally came to him, but it was a fitful sleep, and about midnight he awakened with the uncanny feeling that someone was watching. Careful to make no move that might disclose his wakefulness, he studied the camp through lowered eyelids. The guard had changed and Hardy sat not ten feet away. He watched the deserter stand, stretch his arms, and look around. Quietly he moved closer until he stood directly over the midshipman. Jim raised his eyes and stared at the weatherbeaten face. He thought he saw the features soften in the pale glow of the fire. Hardy seemed on the verge of speaking.

Jim darted his eyes around the camp and saw that he and Hardy were not the only ones awake. Cruet's beady eyes were on the two of them.

For a moment, the midshipman's heart pounded with fear. If Hardy meant to tell him something, Cruet would see the exchange. He flicked his eyes back to the helmsman and then again to Cruet.

Hardy's face underwent an immediate change. He snarled an oath and lashed out with his heavy sea boot to kick the young officer savagely.

"Yer sleepin' too sound, Mr. Murdock," he growled. "Hang me if I don't hate t' see you comfortable!"

Hardy turned and stomped back to the fire, muttering curses.

Jim reached down and rubbed his leg where the man had kicked him. He was more confused than ever. He

could have sworn Hardy's face showed nothing but concern as he stood over him.   Perhaps he had caught Jim's
look of alarm when he saw Cruet watching them.   Or was
the kick an expression of long-suppressed hate for all
officers?   Jim didn't know.   He looked across the fire and
saw Cruet grinning at his discomfort.   That's one thing
I'm sure about, thought Jim: Cruet certainly hates us.

★

CHAPTER 8

Prison

EARLY morning sun brought relief from the chill of the night, but it also brought increased apprehension. Barnum was in even worse shape for the day's trip than on the previous morning. Jim stood up, stretching his cramped legs, then helped the wounded man to his feet. Barnum grimaced with pain every time he moved his arm.

"She sure is swole up," the sailor said, with alarm.

"It'll be all right, Barnum," said Jim. "Just make up your mind you're going to stick it out today, no matter how bad it hurts."

Jim looked across the camp, to see whether the pirates were ready to start, and saw Cruet and his men studying the broad savannah below with intense interest. Obviously, none of the band was anxious to leave the security of the mountains and encounter the enemy army.

One of the pirates gave a cry and pointed to some slender ribbons of smoke rising from the valley. Jim moved closer to the edge of the ledge and took a better look. Must be the breakfast fires of the troops, he thought.

Cruet apparently thought so too. He gave a satisfied grunt then turned to face the midshipman.

"We cross the savannah today," he said. "Your 'ands I free again. But leesten careful, mon petit. Wan false move, wan loud talk, an' we tie you lak peeg and stuff the shirt een the mouth."

"Let me boil some water to treat Barnum's arm before we go, Cruet," Jim demanded.

The pirate stared at the swollen arm. "Non! Non! I 'ave tol' you he die anyway," he replied and turned abruptly away.

Jim felt a wave of pity as he saw Barnum's face blanch. He took him by the good arm. "We'll show the devil," he said. "I promise you'll live to make him wish he'd never seen us."

Jim would never forget his trip that day across the lush savannah. The journey offered the contrasts of incredible beauty and utter desolation. Once-beautiful plantations now lay in ashes in the wake of a vengeful army. Occasionally the group passed a home and saw the bodies of the inhabitants sprawled grotesquely among the ashes. The fly-infested remnants of a once happy family attracted their share of repulsive carrion-eaters, and hundreds of scraggy-necked buzzards had flocked to the valley. To see them at their hideous work was dreadful, nauseating!

Cruet seemed entirely unaffected by the scene. Living in the blood-drenched land had apparently armored his emotions against death in any form. Obviously he took this route through the ravaged area in the hope that Toussaint's army would have nothing to return for.

During the worst heat of the afternoon the pirates halted before a cluster of palm-thatched huts. Situated in a shallow ravine between two forests, the army had either missed or purposely neglected to fire the poor abodes.

Jim helped Barnum into a comfortable spot in the

shade of a palm tree then picked up a broken coconut shell and headed for a small stream some dozen paces away.

Weary as he was, he could not help but admire the beauty of the rather isolated spot. In the nearby forest he recognized cedar, oak and mahogany trees among the ever-present ceibas. Hundreds of small birds were on every hand; in the forest he caught flashes of yellow and green as colorful parrots flew screaming from tree to tall tree.

When he dropped to his knees and scooped up a shellful of water, a ground dove nearby cooed softly and slipped into hiding among the ferns. A carpenter bird on the trunk of a nearby icaco tree left off his boring long enough to regard the midshipman with suspicion. The old expression "free as a bird" crossed Jim's mind. He sighed, shook off the feeling of depression, scooped up another shellful of water for his companions and carried it back to the palm tree.

"Drink this, Barnum, and you'll feel like a new man," he said heartily, as he helped the quartermaster to a sitting position.

"I'd give a lot to feel like a new man, sir." Barnum managed a feeble smile. He drank greedily of the water.

"How much farther do you think we have to go, Mr. Murdock?" asked Hews. He had long since discarded his tattered shirt, several strips of which he'd wound around his head. With his ragged pants and sweating naked torso, the sailor was scarcely distinguishable from one of the pirates.

"We must have covered ten miles through the mountains yesterday," Jim calculated, "and we surely made another ten so far today. I'd say we'll reach Jacmel by late afternoon tomorrow, at the rate we're traveling."

Barnum rolled his eyes toward the pirates who began

to munch on tough strips of dried meat. "Maybe I could make it if they'd give us some food," he said.

Jim stood up and resolutely walked the few paces to the group of pirates. He demanded food and was tossed a few scraps. Meager as it was, it would be a help, he thought, and hurried back to his two companions.

While they sat chewing on the meat, Jim noticed Cruet beckon to one of his men and point to a nearby knoll. The man wiped greasy hands on his filthy breeches and started reluctantly for the rise. Cruet was mighty careful, he thought, even though the army had passed through here the day before. He idly wondered what would happen to them if they were captured by Toussaint's army. Although the United States was actually co-operating with Toussaint, he wondered how much of the diplomatic situation was known to the armies in the field.

Suddenly he heard a startled exclamation from one of the pirates near Cruet and saw him point toward the knoll. He looked and saw the scout running toward the camp at breakneck speed. The man was obviously terror-stricken, and when he stopped before Cruet to gasp out his intelligence, the midshipman saw the other pirates stiffen with fright.

Cruet snapped a series of orders to set the men in motion. Three of them headed for the Americans and quickly tied their hands behind them. "What's goin' on?" Hews asked, in confusion.

One of the pirates cuffed the gunner's mate in answer. All three prisoners were forced to their feet and hurried into the forest at knife point.

Once in the dense undergrowth, their captors tripped and quickly gagged them, threatening them to be quiet or be killed.

A moment after the gag had been jammed into his mouth, Jim saw the pirates stiffen, and he could hear the unmistakable sound of many horses in the distance. He twisted his body around and found he could see a portion of the open area through the underbrush.

Suddenly a resplendent figure on a pure white horse rode into his limited view. The horse stopped, and as the rider swung around, Jim saw one of the ugliest faces he had ever seen. Jet-black, with a bullethead and beady piercing eyes, the squat rider in a dazzling uniform of creamy white had a face of utter cruelty. One by one Jim watched other horsemen ride into view, some black and others so white as to be unrecognizable as mulattoes.

"Dessalines!" he heard one pirate whisper hoarsely, his voice filled with terror at the very name.

Jim's heart pounded. Jean Jacques Dessalines! Toussaint's greatest general! His eyes searched wildly for a means of attracting attention. Near his feet a worm-eaten log leaned precariously against the trunk of a tree. He inched slowly toward it, body taut with excitement. If he could but kick it, surely the horsemen not fifty yards away would investigate the noise.

All at once a pirate was on him, silent as a jungle cat, his face twisted with fear. He dug the point of his knife into the midshipman's chest. Jim stiffened as the sharp blade sent an excruciating pain through his body. The pirate, his eyes showing naked fear and rage, glowered at the young officer.

Jim saw no more. Lying tense against the pain of the knife, he heard the horsemen move out with loud creakings of leather and accouterments and pounding of hoofs. Not until all sounds of the staff and troop had died away, did his assailant remove the knife and stand up.

Jim sat up and looked down at his chest. Blood welled out of the knife cut and rolled down his body to his belt.

"Ees good way to die, Meestaire Murdock."

Cruet stood over the midshipman in hesitation.

Jim said nothing. He got to his feet and faced the pirate captain. If they had anything more in store for him, he wanted to be on his feet.

Cruet regarded him silently for a moment, as if undecided. Finally he turned to his men and said, "We waste time, my cheeldren. Let us move quickly."

Badly shaken by their narrow escape, the pirates set a grueling pace for the remainder of the afternoon. Now Jim could see that they headed directly for the mountain range. Even with his scant knowledge of the country he realized Jacmel was on the other side of that forbidding range. Bone-tired with the constant effort of keeping Barnum on his feet, he had to grit his teeth and exert all his will to keep moving. Once, during the late afternoon, Cruet threatened to leave Barnum on the trail. Jim knew the pirate could readily carry out this threat; nothing could induce Cruet to remain on the plain throughout the night with Dessalines' army so near.

Not until the small party had penetrated deep into a ravine between two mountains did Cruet finally call a halt. No fire was permitted until the pirates scouted the entire surrounding area. Even then, a tiny fire sufficient only for cooking a meager meal was all Cruet would allow.

Although it was long after dark before the tired Americans dropped into an exhausted sleep, Cruet awakened them hours before dawn and forced them to take the trail again. Barnum, feverish and delirious, babbled incoherently as Jim and Hews practically carried him between them. Jim started giving him sharp orders to walk or climb as the trail required, and the quartermaster, accustomed to obeying commands all his adult life, subconsciously obeyed and kept moving.

Near noon, the party rounded the side of a mountain, and Jim's eyes widened in amazed relief. Below, the Caribbean stretched its endless blue surface to a faraway hazy horizon. At the head of a small bay down the mountain slope, the town of Jacmel lay all white and pink in the hot sun. Jim offered a silent prayer that Barnum had been able to last so long.

Cruet's old confidence returned now that he was in sight of his superior's headquarters. Motioning the rest of the party to wait, he strutted down the trail toward a group of soldiers on guard duty. He was met by one who wore a white coat, so dirty that from a distance it looked gray.

In spite of Cruet's superior air, the guard was singularly unimpressed. He did not lower his musket, topped by an enormously long bayonet, until the pirate established his identity. Even then, the sergeant—for Jim recognized him as such by his chevrons—showed little respect. He returned with Cruet to the waiting group, glanced at the obviously penniless prisoners, and listlessly waved the party on.

Very shortly the trail gave way to a road, and the three Americans began to catch glimpses of the luxurious villas overlooking the town. It was evident that the owners were or had been enormously wealthy. To the tired prisoners, the wide verandas opening onto beautifully kept terraces of velvet grass were a paradise on earth.

By the time they reached the stone-paved plaza in the center of town, Jim began to see an occasional Frenchman in uniform. He realized the French were secretly backing Rigaud in his struggle against Toussaint L'Ouverture, but he hadn't expected to see uniformed officers of the French Army openly strolling in the streets.

As crowds of townspeople began to gather and watch the prisoners march by, Jim glanced at Hardy to see if the deserter was enjoying his shipmates' humiliation. If he was, he gave no sign. The former helmsman walked steadily along, stony-faced and without any apparent interest in the crowds.

Passing on through the town, the party followed the shoreline of the bay to a large squat building. Jim saw a few windows in the wooden structure, all heavily barred. The unpainted eyesore lay close, but not right upon the shore. The building was situated on a sandspit reaching into the marsh. Hemmed in on three sides by the marsh grass and occasional patches of canebrake, it represented a dismal picture.

On their arrival at a great double door, or gate, in the front, Cruet spoke to a guard slumped against the wall. The soldier banged against the gate with the butt of his musket. After a long wait, a face appeared in a small opening that was covered with an iron grille. Pockmarked and dirty, the face was evil and repulsive. When it withdrew after a careful inspection of the group, Jim heard sounds of a bar being removed then saw one of the heavy gates swing open. A squad of soldiers moved out, surrounded the three Americans and forced them into the prison at bayonet point. Jim had time to look over his shoulder. His eyes singled out Hardy. The former helmsman met his gaze for a few seconds, then looked away. This is just what you wanted, Hardy, he thought, bitterly. He could not stand the sight of the renegade!

Jim recognized the interior of the building as slave-pens built by those despicable traffickers in human flesh.

The malodorous swamp smelled like incense compared to the stench under the hot roof. On all hands he could hear moans of desperately sick men. As they passed the tiny cells, the haggard faces of men without hope appeared at each tiny barred opening, high on the doors.

Finally the guards halted before a cell, kicked open the door and pushed Barnum and Hews in. Hews fought off the guards when he saw Jim was not coming in and ran back to the midshipman.

"I ain't goin' in there without you, sir," he cried.

The pock-marked jailer brought up the butt of his musket and with a curse swung it into the side of the gunner's mate's head. Hews' knees buckled. He tried to grab Jim's arm but fell unconscious before he could reach him.

"You devil!" yelled Jim. With a sweep of his arm he brushed aside the nearest bayonet and lunged at the guard standing over Hews. He threw a wild right that caught the soldier just under the chin.

Slowly the whole squad lowered their bayonets and approached him warily. Forming a rude semicircle, the razor-sharp points forced him back against the wall. Ringed in and helpless, he watched two guards close in and pinion his arms behind his back. The pock-marked guard approached, his eyes blazing with rage. Deliberately he cocked his right arm and sent his fist smashing into Jim's face.

★

CHAPTER 9

Angélique

JIM sat on the dirt floor of the darkened cell, holding his aching head. For a moment he could do nothing because of the ringing in his ears. He moved his jaw tentatively and found it was not broken. He looked up, his eyes seeking a small window, the only source of light in the cell. With something to focus on, his head cleared rapidly.

"My young friend, I trust you aren't seriously hurt."

Jim started, then looked around the room to locate the sound of the voice. He made out the figure of another prisoner leaning against the wall, in the corner. As he stared the figure moved forward into the light to disclose a slender, erect individual dressed in a well-tailored gray linen suit, showing traces of its former elegance. The man's wavy black hair, touched with gray at the temples, topped an alert and distinguished face. His steady eyes showed concern for the young officer's predicament.

"I guess I'm all right now," Jim said, and rose unsteadily to his feet.

"It is not difficult to place your nationality, mon ami. Only an American would so rashly attack the guards of this establishment." His eyes traveled over the weary but sturdy shoulders of the midshipman. "In fact you are quite fortunate to be alive. But let me introduce myself—M. Émile Moreau, at your service, sir."

"Glad to meet you, Mr. Moreau," said Jim. "I'm Jim Murdock, late midshipman in the United States Navy."

"You must have a long story to tell, Jim. I hope to hear it in detail. But first let me get you some food and drink."

Jim raised his eyebrows. "Food, sir?"

"I have the status, for the moment, of privileged guest, Jim," Moreau explained. "How long that status will continue, I have no idea." He retrieved a box from the corner of the cell, placed it on the floor in front of the midshipman and threw back the lid. "Biscuits and a flagon of mild wine. It is poor fare, but will allay your hunger. I can offer you much better tomorrow, I hope."

Between bites, Jim told his new friend of his capture and subsequent adventures with General Rigaud's pirates, under their leader, Antoine Cruet.

"I have heard of him, this Captain Cruet," Moreau said. "A despicable and rapacious creature. As a result of his successes against shipping in St. Marc Channel, he has, however, endeared himself to Rigaud."

"Aye, he's been successful, all right," agreed Jim. "He's kept half the squadron pinned down to convoy duty by his raiding barges."

M. Moreau pursed his lips and stared thoughtfully at Jim. "This is not so good, no? Nothing succeeds with Rigaud like success. He has certainly experienced a dearth of it with his army."

"With the capture of a fine brig like the *Rover* he'll really be in a good position, I guess," said Jim. He frowned, sighed and added, "It would appear that Cruet will have a great deal to say about our fate."

"Now that General Rigaud is pressed by the forces of Toussaint, I would say yes," the man replied.

"Then if Cruet wants to do away with us, he can?"
Jim questioned.

"To be blunt, yes," said Moreau. "But I believe that
possibility does not exist, my friend. Alive and well,
you represent a valuable asset to Rigaud. First, in the
matter of prestige alone, you are the first American officer
captured by his forces." Moreau held up his hand in a
gesture of apology as he saw the midshipman wince. "I
do not mean to hurt your feelings, Jim, I merely state a
fact. Is it not so?"

Jim nodded.

"Second," continued the older man, "alive, you may be
used to purchase the freedom of one or more of Rigaud's
officers now held by the American Navy." He shrugged.
"Enfin, it would be useless to eliminate you or your
friends."

"Holy Moses!" exclaimed Jim suddenly. He ran to
the tiny opening in the cell door and looked out.

"What is it, Jim?" asked Moreau, alarmed by the midshipman's obvious agitation. "Why are you so concerned?"

Jim whirled to face the Frenchman. "Hews and Barnum, sir! Did you see where the guards took them?
Barnum's sick. He needs a doctor!"

"Not so fast, Jim. Your friends, yes. I saw the guards
throw them in the adjoining cell." He pointed to one
wall. "They are on the other side of those planks."

Jim ran to the wall and examined the heavy boards.
He could see where they had warped in places to permit
rather wide cracks.

"Hews," he called in a low voice. "Can you hear me,
Hews?"

From the other side of the wall came a muffled, "Aye,
sir."

"How is Barnum?" Jim asked anxiously.

"He ain't doin' so well, Mr. Murdock. Them guards shook him up quite a bit." There was silence for a moment, then Hews went on, "He don't know what's goin' on any more, sir. He's feverish and mumblin' wildlike to himself. I don't reckon there's any use takin' the bandage off; I ain't got nothin' to fix it with, anyway."

"Do you have any water?" asked Jim.

"We don't have nothin', sir."

Jim turned from the wall. The hopelessness of their predicament engulfed him like a wave. All of his efforts to keep Barnum alive had been for nothing.

"Mr. Murdock."

Jim turned to the crack in the planks.

"Yes."

"It's sure good to know you're so close," said Hews.

Jim hesitated before answering. He straightened his shoulders. These men were depending on him. He was a fool to give way to self-pity. "Keep up your spirit," he said. "Try to keep Barnum as comfortable as possible. I'll get him help, some way."

"Your friend," said Moreau, sympathetically. "He is sick from fever?"

Jim glanced at his cell mate as if he had forgotten he was in the room. He had been so preoccupied with his thoughts of Barnum's condition he had, for the moment, thought of nothing else.

"Worse than that, sir. Barnum took a ball in his arm. He's had no proper treatment for it, and I'm afraid infection has taken hold." Jim clenched his fists. "I've got to get help for him! I've got to!"

"Do not despair, my friend," said Moreau. "Perhaps I can be of some help."

Jim looked up, his eyes full of hope. "You're a doctor?"

"No," said Moreau, "but I expect a caller." He smiled at Jim's look of astonishment. "I told you I was a favored prisoner. This caller," Moreau continued, "will undoubtedly be one Lieutenant Visseau of the French Navy, fortunately a surgeon."

"A French surgeon in Jacmel?"

"It is difficult to understand, I know. France supports, as quietly as possible, the efforts of General Rigaud." Moreau shrugged expressively. "Why? One finds politics so unaccountably confused, particularly here in this unfortunate country. But, nevertheless, I feel certain I can prevail on the good lieutenant to look at your friend."

"Are you sure?" asked Jim. After all, the French had no love for the Americans. Particularly right now.

"I feel certain he will." Moreau smiled. "Now let's not be so glum, my young friend. Explain to your friends that there is room for hope. Perhaps it will give the wounded man strength to face the morrow."

Jim hurried to the cell wall. He hesitated, then turned to Moreau again. "You think he'll be here soon?"

"No later than tomorrow noon, of a certainty."

When Jim wakened the next morning, he felt more refreshed than he had for days. Aside from an angry bruise on his cheek, a memento of the pock-marked guard's brutal blow, there was little to show that he was not his robust self again.

Moreau was certainly a godsend, he thought. He had learned a little of the man's background the night before. A wealthy Creole, the name applied to Frenchmen born outside France, he owned several productive plantations. He was held now on a flimsy charge of having sheltered Toussaint's troops on one of his plantations; flimsy indeed, since the various armies in the country took what they wanted anyway. Moreau explained the matter as a political one stemming from both jealousy and greed. Although Rigaud·was disposed to look on Moreau with favor, the Moreau family had excited the animosity of one of the general's army commanders. The consequence of the situation was that Moreau was imprisoned, but because of his wealth and his influence in France, Rigaud allowed him certain favors permitted no other prisoners.

Moreau spoke little of his family, and Jim, not knowing what they had suffered, was reluctant to ask. He admired the slender but wiry man tremendously. His very presence had done much to give Jim hope.

Jim, having finished a biscuit for breakfast instead of the greasy mess handed in through the hole in the door, looked over to his cell mate who was just finishing his own meagre meal.

"Do you think, sir—" began Jim.

"Yes, my impatient young friend. Lieutenant Visseau will be here. Have no fear."

Even as he spoke, Jim heard voices outside the cell door. A moment later the sergeant of the guard's ugly face filled the opening in the door. The midshipman backed away as he heard the bolt shoot free.

Suddenly the door flew open, almost knocking him down. He caught a glimpse of a vision in white running across the cell and saw a young girl throw herself into Moreau's arms.

"Papa! Oh, papa!" the girl cried, as she smothered her father with kisses.

"Angélique, ma chérie," Moreau murmured.

Jim's attention was diverted by a second person entering the cell. Tall, handsome, the man was dressed in the uniform of the French Navy. Jim watched him observing the reunion of father and daughter with compassion in his eyes.

The officer caught sight of Jim. He ran his eyes up and down the midshipman's sturdy figure with a cold eye. He started to speak, but Moreau put in quickly.

"My dear Visseau. How good of you to come." Holding Angélique in one arm, he extended the other hand to the French officer. "I am deeply grateful that you were able to bring my child to see me."

"And it is good to see you again," Visseau answered. He nodded in Jim's direction. "I will have that prisoner assigned to another cell."

"But no!" Moreau's eyes darted to the American. "Jim! How forgetful of me. Come," he led his daughter toward the midshipman, "come, ma chérie, and meet my young American friend."

On high-heel slippers of white kid, Angélique seemed to glide rather than walk as she approached the young officer. Although not five feet tall she seemed taller because of her erect carriage.

For a moment Jim could find no words. With the squalid walls of the former slavepen as a background, the sight of the beautiful young girl left him speechless. Although he knew he stared, he could not take his eyes from the lovely face, lustrous white in the dim light of the cell. Only when her long lashes fell under his frank scrutiny did he remember his manners. Acutely aware of his ragged and half-naked appearance, he began to blush furiously.

"Angélique, my dear, and Lieutenant Visseau, may I present Mr. Murdock, midshipman in the American Navy."

"M'sieu," murmured Angélique, and dropped a curtsey.

Feeling as awkward as any country bumpkin, Jim stammered, "A p-pleasure, ma'am," and bowed with all the dignity he could muster.

"I am so happy papa has a friend in this—this unspeakable place." She turned and threw herself again into her father's arms.

"There, there, my pet. I am not suffering. Why," he threw out his hands in an expressive gesture, "aside from the inconvenience of imprisonment I am treated very well."

Lieutenant Visseau spoke up. "Believe me, m'sieu, I plead your case daily with General Rigaud. Without raising your hopes too much, I think I am making progress. Please believe me, sir."

"I am sure you exhaust yourself in my behalf," Moreau answered, generously.

Jim shot a quick glance at the French officer. How immaculate he appeared in his gleaming white uniform. He found himself envying the man his cleanliness. Suddenly he thought of Barnum.

"Sir," he said to Moreau. "If the lieutenant—"

"But of course, Jim! Forgive me," he said, anticipating Jim's request. He turned to Visseau and quickly explained the seriousness of the American sailor's condition.

Jim saw the surgeon frown, his face assuming a grave professional look.

"I shall attend to it at once, m'sieu," he said, when the

Creole had finished his explanation. He walked to the open cell door and called loudly for the sergeant of the guards.

"Open the next cell while I attend the sick American," he ordered.

The guard scowled fiercely.

"It is not permitted!" he said.

Jim watched Visseau's hand fall to his sword hilt.

"I have a pass to visit this prison." The lieutenant's voice was cold as ice. "It is signed by his excellency, the general. It is unlimited in scope. You will open the next cell, Sergeant. Do you understand?" He drew his sword a few inches from the scabbard. "Nothing, Sergeant, would give me greater pleasure than to spit you as I would a pig."

The sergeant's face blanched. He stared in terrified fascination at the few inches of bright blade above the scabbard. He darted fearful eyes at the lieutenant's granitelike face, then commenced to fumble at a ring of keys in his rope belt.

Jim turned to Moreau when the French surgeon stalked out of the cell behind the guard. "I can't begin to thank you, sir," he said.

"It is little enough, Jim." He waved aside any thanks. "Let us hope your man has received aid in time."

Angélique faced Jim, her lovely eyes troubled. "Is there anything I can do, M. Murdock? Perhaps—" she ran to the wicker basket she had dropped on the threshold as she entered the cell. "Perhaps we can share this food and wine with your countrymen."

"Bless you, ma'am," Jim said gratefully. "And I'm sure Barnum and Hews will, too."

Jim was under a spell as he listened to the girl's animated chatter. The minutes flew by, and it seemed but a moment before the French lieutenant entered their cell once again.

The surgeon's sensitive eyes sought out Jim's.

"I would not alarm you, Mr. Murdock, but your man is seriously ill. The fever—the infection—both have taken hold." He pursed his lips thoughtfully. "Of course these seamen have iron constitutions. If we can keep the infection localized, I believe he will recover. I have dressed the wound and will return tomorrow to care for it again." He turned to Angélique. "And now, mam'selle, I think we had best leave." He walked toward the door.

"Lieutenant, I am deeply grateful," said Jim.

"It is nothing, Mr. Murdock," said Visseau. "I am attached to the staff of General Rigaud, yes. But this is because my country has so ordered it. I am not required to act like a savage like these—" He broke off the sentence realizing Angélique was present.

"I will be with you in a minute, m'sieu," said Angélique.

Jim watched the girl embrace her father again and saw her whisper urgently into his ear. Moreau started a protest, but Angélique stopped him with a quick kiss, then darted a look at the cell door to see if Visseau was watching. Assuring herself that the lieutenant had stepped outside, she thrust her hand inside her father's coat. Jim caught a flash of metal in the brief second her hand moved. He quickly averted his eyes and walked toward the door.

Angélique turned from her father, eyes glistening, and said, "I am so happy, m'sieu, that papa is no longer alone." She walked over to the midshipman and laid a hand on his arm. "You will assist papa, will you not?"

Jim stared down into the round lovely eyes and stam-

mered, "In—in any way I can." What he really meant
was that he would move the nearest mountain if she
desired it.

Not until Angélique had been gone for fully a minute
did he start guiltily and turn to see Moreau watching
with amusement.

"A bewitching child, is she not, my friend?"

"Sir," said Jim, fervently, "she's the loveliest lady I've
ever met."

"Ah, Jim. I'm afraid she has snared you, too. For a
child of fifteen, Angélique draws too many admirers.
They moon like calves on our veranda every day."

"Did you say fifteen, sir? Why I thought—"

"You will learn, Jim, that even young ladies seem
grown-up here. Many of Angélique's girl friends are now
married." He shrugged. "I for one do not think this
is right but—" He pulled a knife from his coat. "Now
the child is playing at intrigue. She has smuggled this
weapon to me that I may fight my way clear, perhaps."
He smiled tolerantly. "Womanly romance, I'm afraid."
He handed the blade to Jim.

The midshipman turned the knife over in his hand,
slowly. Obviously of good steel, the edge was razor-sharp.
He looked up at Moreau.

"Maybe Angélique's gift will be of more help than
you realize," said Jim, thoughtfully.

★

CHAPTER 10

General Rigaud

IT WAS NOT until the third day after Lieutenant Visseau's first visit that Barnum showed any real improvement. The Frenchman tended the wound every day. In the meantime, however, Jim had not been idle. Using Moreau's knife, he had worked loose one end of a heavy plank on the cell wall. By pulling on this end, he could spring the board far enough to pass food through to the sailors.

That third morning, Visseau stopped in Jim's cell to report Barnum on the way to recovery, barring any complications. He also left a basket of food Angélique had prepared. If he suspected they were getting food to the sailors he made no mention of it. Jim thought his eyes searched the cell wall uncommonly long, but put it down to mere suspicion on his part.

Moreau flatly refused to doubt the lieutenant's loyalty to the Moreau family.

"Visseau would never concern himself about this matter, Jim. You are unduly alarmed, my boy," he said.

"Maybe you're right, sir, but after all, he is on the general's staff."

Moreau shrugged. "A matter of politics. Rigaud has many influential friends in France. While the Republic sends many such 'volunteers' to aid the cause of the rebellion, Napoleon honors Toussaint and his officers

with rank of general in the French Army. It is a dangerous game. France hopes to be on the winning side in
any event."

"But Toussaint must know of this," said Jim.

"Of course. L'Ouverture is a master of intrigue himself. He is willing to close his eyes to France's duplicity
for the time being. Toussaint, however, was a slave but
a few years ago. He would let all his armies be annihilated
rather than become a slave again. He will never surrender, and the people love him and will die for him."

"But what of you and your family? Where do the
whites fit into the picture?"

"Ah, that is difficult to say, Jim. As to my family,
there is but Angélique and myself; her mother long ago
died of the fever." He stared up at the shaft of light
entering the room through the little window. "As to the
future of the blancs, or whites, if Toussaint can establish
peace in the country he will permit them to stay. I doubt,
though, that their plantations will be returned. On the
other hand, if Rigaud and his faction win, perhaps they
too would welcome the whites for the sake of business."
He thought for a moment. "My own feeling is this: the
hatreds are too deep-seated for this land to enjoy any
real peace."

"But you, sir," said Jim. "What will Rigaud do with
you and—and Angélique?"

"Have no concern, my friend," said Moreau, confidently. "Rigaud will certainly keep me alive until he
locates my reputed fortune. And that he will never do.
With regard to Angélique, the French on Rigaud's staff
will never permit harm to come to her. Visseau and the
others will see to that."

Jim couldn't believe the matter to be as simple as
his friend put it. No matter which side won the war,

Moreau stood to lose everything. Though he believed himself but a political prisoner, he was nonetheless in great danger. With the politics of the island in its present confused state, no one could say for a certainty what would happen the next day. If Dessalines, Toussaint's general in the south, decided to drive on Jacmel, the town would become a bloody battlefield.

With this thought in mind, Jim walked to the corner of the cell and uncovered the knife, buried in the dirt floor. With its point he began working on a plank between the cells. Fortunately, the slavepens were never designed for more than a temporary housing for slaves, and little care had gone into the building's construction. He pried loose one end of a heavy plank and called to Hews.

"Yes, sir. Barnum's feeling much better already." Hews nodded to the quartermaster who, for the first time since their imprisonment, sat with his back to the wall.

Barnum raised his eyes and managed a weak smile. "I'll be right as rain in a few days, sir."

"Of course you will, man," Jim answered heartily.

Hews moved closer to the open board. "Have you any plans, sir?" he asked, in a whisper.

"You mean plans for escape?"

The gunner's mate craned his neck and shot a quick look through the small opening to locate Jim's cell mate. He questioned the midshipman with his eyes.

"You can trust Mr. Moreau," said Jim.

"I been lookin' around, sir," Hews said. "With that little knife of yours I think I can loosen the boards on the outside wall."

"But what good would that do? The swamps are on all three sides of the prison. You couldn't get away even if we did get out."

"I wouldn't mind a little swamp much, sir. And

anyway, there's about ten feet of sand up close to the out-side wall," explained Hews. "If we went around to the sea side of the prison, we'd only have about a hundred yards of swamp to cover to get to open water. We could swim from there."

"Swim to where?"

Hews looked perplexed. "Well, I don't rightly know, but surely we could swim past the swamp and maybe get back into the hills."

Jim shook his head. "We'd be out of our minds to head for the hills. The back country's crawling with soldiers. We couldn't get a day's journey without getting caught." He started to say more, but a warning hiss from Moreau galvanized him into action. He quickly let the board spring into place and turned to face the door. He leaned casually against the wall.

"Guard's coming," Moreau whispered. "Throw me the knife."

Jim tossed the knife to the older man who quickly thrust it into his waistcoat.

A second later Jim saw the sergeant's ugly face appear at the opening. After a quick look the face disappeared, and Jim heard the bolt shot back.

Two soldiers swung open the door and entered the cell, their bayoneted muskets at the ready. Immediately following them a light-skinned officer stepped briskly into the cell. His eyes singled out the midshipman.

"Murdock, you will follow me."

His eyebrows arched in contempt as he surveyed the American's tattered uniform. "The slightest resistance and my men will shoot you down. Do you understand?"

Jim nodded. He looked questioningly at Moreau.

Moreau shrugged. "It is perhaps an interrogation. Do not be apprehensive."

Jim squared his shoulders. He felt his stomach muscles contract. His mouth felt unaccountably dry. What was in store for him, he could only guess. And his guess did not please him.

He walked through the door and saw a whole squad of well-armed soldiers lined up in the passageway. The officer pointed and Jim commenced walking to the front gate of the prison.

The bright sunlight on the hot white sand almost blinded him when the two heavy doors swung open. The soldiers formed a boxlike square around him and headed toward the town.

When his eyes became accustomed to the glare of midday, Jim took the opportunity to look around. He noted a feverish activity, contrasting strangely with the appearance of the town the day Cruet delivered him to the prison. On two occasions the squad moved to one side of the narrow street to clear a path for a troop of cavalry, riding at full gallop through the town. Soldiers were at every corner, mounting guard over hastily improvised barricades. When the squad reached the plaza he saw new recruits drilling, their French-type kepis askew and their uniforms drenched with perspiration.

The squad moved on past the center of town and up the slope overlooking the harbor. Jim heard the soldiers around him commence to breathe heavily. He was glad for once he didn't have to carry a heavy musket and bayonet. He took a deep breath of the warm, flower-scented air and fixed his eyes on a gleaming white villa just ahead. Placed in the center of a deep green terrace, the dazzling white structure was the most imposing he had seen on the island. Roof-high columns ran across the entire front of the villa. Behind these he saw a wide veranda filled with animated and gesturing officers in a wide variety of colorful uniforms.

Jim realized to his surprise the villa was their destination when the squad entered the grounds on a seashell driveway. Before they reached the veranda, the officer-in-charge barked a command. The squad halted. The officer motioned to Jim to step forward.

"His excellency, General Rigaud, wishes to speak to you." He drew a pistol from the yellow sash at his waist and leveled the muzzle at Jim's chest. "I will be right behind you. You will make no untoward movement in the presence of his excellency."

Jim eyed the young officer coldly, looked up the drive then commenced to walk slowly toward the villa. When the officers gathered at the villa caught sight of him, the talking subsided. He knew he was the object of stares and whispers but paid no attention. He couldn't help but wish he wore his best uniform, or at least a clean and complete one, yet he ignored the stares and reminded himself that tattered as his present dress was, he represented the United States Navy. He set his face and deliberately surveyed the surroundings, noticed the well-kept palms and pepper trees lining the driveway, then let his eyes wander to the scene below. On the blue and green surface of the bay he could see an uncommon number of ships anchored offshore. While it was impossible to recognize their flags at this distance, he identified several French ships by their rakish lines. Of far greater interest were two ships apparently patrolling—they carried little canvas—well offshore. How he wished for a long glass to see if they were American.

The officer prodded him with his pistol and pointed to the veranda. Jim brought his thoughts back to the

situation at hand.   He faced half left, walked between
the columns into the cool depths of the veranda and came
to stop before an overdressed general, so obviously the
center of fawning attention by the others, that Jim knew
he could be none other than Rigaud.

His excellency, General Rigaud, supreme commander
of the southern portion of the island, fancied himself the
New World's greatest general.   Faultlessly dressed in a
white uniform, the collar of which touched his ear lobes,
he stood fingering an imposing array of medals and dec-
orations virtually covering his chest.   His shiny black
boots reached well above his knees.   A crimson sash
around his waist added color to the uniform, but the lace
handkerchief tucked in it made his whole appearance
foppish.   His hair was long, jet-black, and curly.   It
framed the light brown face to give the general a look of
femininity.   With his graceful movements and gestures,
Jim thought one could easily take him for a comic opera
general, that is until you looked into his eyes—eyes that
reflected coldness and cruelty.

Jim stood straight before the general, and as Rigaud
stared at him, the midshipman had a curious feeling that
his captor instinctively hated him.   A full head taller than
the general, he realized the man had to look up and sensed
that this irked the supreme commander.

"American," Rigaud said, "if you answer my questions correctly, I may find it convenient to have you
exchanged."

Jim said nothing but stared straight ahead.

The contemptuous smile on Rigaud's face vanished.

"I am told you were an officer on the American ship
Victory. What were your orders regarding Jacmel?" he
demanded.

Jim thought quickly. If he refused to answer the question, he and his companions might well be tortured. In Barnum's present condition this could prove fatal. He was determined to evade direct answers if at all possible.

"As a junior officer you would hardly expect my captain to confide in me," he replied.

"To what port was the *Victory* sailing?"

"Our orders, so far as I know, were to escort merchantmen. As to what port we would ultimately make, I am not in a position to say."

Rigaud's eyes narrowed. "What do you mean! In no position to say! Do you know or don't you?"

"I have already told you," Jim replied steadily, "my commanding officer was not in the habit of confiding in me." An understatement, thought the midshipman, if I've ever heard one.

Rigaud sniffed in disgust. He pulled the scented handkerchief from his waist and held it to his nose, at the same time distastefully running his eyes up and down the American's clothing.

Jim flushed at the obvious appraisal.

Rigaud spoke again: "What were the orders of the squadron under Captain Talbot with regard to French ships?"

Jim noticed a quick interest lighten the faces of several French officers in the group.

"Ships of the United States Navy need no orders to fire on any foreign ship exhibiting signs of hostility," Jim answered, his eyes steady on the general.

"Oh, take him away," Rigaud pouted, and turned to the others. "This boy knows nothing. I am convinced he is but a crude fool, at best."

The staff officers tittered and broke into smiles, nodding their heads in quick agreement.

"With your permission, mon général."

Jim saw a movement at the rear of the group and watched an officer push his way to the front.

Rigaud arched his eyebrows and turned to see who caused the interruption. Recognizing the officer, he said, "Ah yes, Admiral. I believe you are not only the captor of this prisoner but the one who claimed he could be a source of much naval intelligence."

Jim stared at the elaborately dressed individual who came to the forefront. It was Cruet. Holy Moses! Cruet an admiral!

Cruet was flushing deeply under the general's cutting remark. Jim watched him stand before Rigaud, his dark blue uniform covered with gold and his shoulders supporting two of the largest epaulets Jim had ever seen. Cruet kept his fore-and-aft full-dress hat on his head with difficulty, and with one hand on it and the other on the hilt of an overlong sword, he presented a most ludicrous picture. In spite of himself Jim could not suppress a smile.

Cruet glanced at the midshipman and caught the smile. Concealing his anger with difficulty, he spoke to Rigaud. "With your permission, mon général, I would ask a question of the américain."

Cruet turned to Jim, a sly look on his face.

"You were capitaine of the prize sheep. You 'ave said you did not know where the *Victory* intended to go. To what port were *you* ordaired to proceed?"

Jim knew by this time Cruet had bragged about his important capture. He had undoubtedly indicated that Jim could reveal much information concerning American intentions in the Caribbean. The pirate was determined

not to have his reputation suffer and had phrased his question to trap the American.

"Why, Admiral," replied Jim blandly, putting faint stress on the title, "my captain directed me to follow the *Victory*."

Jim heard one of the officers in the background giggle. Cruet's face twitched with suppressed emotion. He collected his wits with effort and turned again to Rigaud.

"I agree, mon général. This one ees a fool."

★

CHAPTER 11

Admiral Cruet

JIM found Moreau pacing the cell, restlessly awaiting his return. The older man could scarcely withhold his questions until the guard closed the door. "Tell me everything that happened, Jim. They are going to exchange you, yes?" Jim shook his head. "I'm afraid not, sir. At least, the general didn't act as if he intended to, by the time he finished questioning me. All he wanted was information." He told Moreau of the conversation.

"And you say this Cruet is now an admiral?" Moreau asked.

Jim smiled. "And about the silliest looking admiral afloat, I'd say."

Moreau frowned and shook his head. "The very fact of his being an admiral shows how high he stands in Rigaud's favor. We cannot discount that." He placed his hand on the midshipman's shoulder. "I would not have recommended this before, but with Cruet in such a position of authority you must seriously consider escape."

"Escape?" Jim asked. He had of course examined that possibility, particularly after Hews had spoken of it earlier. Until now, it was out of the question; Barnum would never have been able to go with them. Now, real planning was possible, since the seaman would be on his feet soon.

"Why yes," Moreau went on. "Your seaman was probably right about the strength of the walls. These old slavepens were never designed to frustrate a well-planned escape. The slave dealers depended more on chains than barriers."

Jim walked to the wall and stared up at the tiny window. On close inspection he saw that the wood holding the iron bars in place was quite old, although sound enough in looks. He stretched his hand upward and found the lower sill just a few inches above his fingertip. Measuring the distance, he jumped, caught the edge and drew himself up until he could see outside. For about a half mile the canebrake extended toward the slopes of nearby hills. Hundreds of small shore birds rose and wheeled and swooped down again. Between the patches of canebrake he could see open areas of dormant, stagnant-appearing water. He wondered vaguely if the population of the swamp included crocodiles, usually a fixture in the swamps of the country. Pulling himself even higher he looked down and sure enough, there appeared to be firm sand close to the wall. He dropped lightly to the floor.

"Hews is right about the sand. It looks solid and extends about ten feet from the prison wall."

"Then you think you might get away if you can get out?"

"Perhaps," answered Jim. "But where would we be then? The terrain's alive with Rigaud's troops, and more of them will be watching the mountain passes for Dessalines' army. I don't think we could get a mile away without being cut down."

Moreau stared thoughtfully at the high window. "Perhaps there is a way, Jim. If someone in town were to arrange for food and weapons, and perhaps a guide . . ."

"You don't mean Angélique?"

"But of course, my boy. Who else? She is very capable and is the soul of discretion—when she so chooses."

"Oh no!" Jim exclaimed. "Why, you can't be serious, sir! If Rigaud found out she helped us, there's no telling what he might do." He shook his head emphatically. "No sir, you're not going to get her mixed up in anything like that!"

"Very well, my boy. But I assure you Angélique would love the intrigue and is a very clever girl. What is more, you need a friend on the outside." He sighed. "Seems a pity. The child would love the adventure and secrecy."

"Maybe so, but I'd rather stay in prison than have her get in trouble for helping us."

Moreau directed a long searching look at the midshipman's earnest face. A slow smile began to form on his lips. "Why, Jim," he said, "I believe the child . . ."

Whatever the Creole intended to say was cut short by a sudden activity outside their door. Amid much shouting and general confusion the two prisoners heard the bolt shot and watched the door swing open.

Two soldiers moved into the cell and backed the prisoners against the wall. At that moment Cruet appeared in the doorway. He looked in carefully, saw the guards holding Jim at bay, then stepped confidently into the cell.

Cruet completely ignored the Creole and approached the midshipman with an affected attitude that reminded Jim of Rigaud's mincing ways.

"M. Murdock," he said sneeringly, "I mus' see eef you 'ave all the comforts." He looked around the bare cell, glanced up at the tiny window, then returned his eyes to the midshipman. "Ees shame, m'sieu, you mus' leeve een thees place. But," he spread his hands dramatically, "what can one do? You 'ave but to answer the questions, an' we fin' a much bettaire place."

"I've answered your questions, and those of General Rigaud," Jim said.

Cruet threw up his hand. "Ah, m'sieu, you may fool mon général, but Antoine Cruet, nevaire. You know where the sheeps of the squadron are place. You tell Cruet an' I see you 'ave plenty food and good quartaires."

"As I said, junior officers know nothing of these matters."

Cruet studied the young midshipman. "You 'ave tol' mon général the lie when you say you do not know where the *Victory* sail. You forget, m'sieu, you once tell me you exchange me off Jacmel. Voilà! So the *Victory* sail for Jacmel, no?"

"I told you before that the captain didn't tell me where we were headed. I offered to exchange you in Jacmel because that's the only place Rigaud could keep any prisoners."

"You lie!" Cruet shouted.

Observing Jim's eyes turn cold as ice, Cruet backed away a step and glanced quickly at the two soldiers to make sure they were alert. Confident once again, he smiled contemptuously.

"I theenk maybe you weel want to answer the questions een two—t'ree days. Een the meantime your sailors get no food or water." He moved away, then to Jim again: "Eef you are ready to talk before, tell the guard."

As soon as the two soldiers slammed the door, Jim walked to the hole and looked out. Assured they were gone he turned to Moreau and smiled.

"Cruet looks almost respectable in that uniform."

Moreau flashed an answering smile, then grew serious. "It's a good thing we can supply your men with food.

This man is dangerous. I'm afraid you underestimate him."

Jim's face clouded. Underestimate Cruet. Never! Would he ever forget the pirate's treatment of Barnum during the trip across country?—the callous murder of his own follower and his feeding him to the barracuda? No, he would never underestimate the man. He answered his cell mate in a low voice. "I don't think you have to worry about that. He's blood brother to a copperhead."

"This copperhead, I do not know what you mean, but . I do know you are in danger. This man wants information of the American squadron, and he will stop at nothing to get it."

"Aye," agreed Jim. "If Cruet knew the patrol stations of the American ships he could avoid them and take more prizes."

"That sounds logical even to me, a landsman," Moreau replied.

"Actually though, I don't know what these positions are. How can Cruet hope to get the information out of me?"

"Perhaps Cruet doesn't realize this. That would make it even more difficult for you. He will torture you for the information. He needs to regain favor with the general. Personally, I think we should direct all our efforts to getting you free."

Jim thought for a minute. "Even if what you say is true, how can we possibly escape in three days? We have but one small knife to work with. We need food and weapons." He paced the tiny cell restlessly. "It will take a great deal of work to get through the outside wall, even if it is old wood."

"Yes, my friend, but three days is a great deal of time when a man is desperate," replied Moreau. "As to food,

I will inform Angélique tomorrow morning. We can have her bring more food on her next trip."

Jim eyed the older man suspiciously. "You know how I feel about Angélique getting mixed up in this. We're not to tell her of the plan to escape."

"This I agree to, Jim. I will tell her of Cruet's orders and the need for more food for your men."

"Which reminds me," said Jim, "I'd better see how Barnum's improving." He glanced at the door. "Will you watch the passage while I loosen the board?"

Moreau nodded and moved quickly to the hole in the door. After a careful look, he motioned an "all clear" to the young officer.

Jim pried the rusty bolts from one end of the loose plank and peered into the next cell.

"Hews," he whispered.

"Aye, sir," the gunner's mate answered.

"How's Barnum faring?"

"I'm in rare form, sir," the quartermaster answered for himself. He moved over to the wall beside Hews.

"It's certainly good to see you on your feet again," said Jim enthusiastically. "How's the arm coming along?"

"It's fine, Mr. Murdock. In another couple of days I can take a turn on any ship's helm."

"Fine, fine," said Jim. "Now listen carefully." He glanced over his shoulder and received a reassuring nod from Moreau. "It looks like we'd better try an escape very soon." He told them of Cruet's visit and his threats.

"We heard a lot of noise and figured someone important had paid you a visit," said Hews. "We didn't know it was that bilge rat, though!"

"We're with you, Mr. Murdock," said Barnum. "I'm well enough to leave right now if you want to. Don't worry none about me, sir."

"I won't, Barnum," Jim said. "Now here's what I plan to do. Although the outside wall is built of heavy timbers, I'm convinced the bolts are rusty and the wood pretty soft in spots. I'll try to loosen a couple of them so we can get through. In the meantime you men try to work loose two or three more boards here, so you can move into this cell when we're ready to leave. We'll leave when it's dark and head up the coast." He paused for a moment. "It's hard to tell how long it will take me to get two planks loose, but let's plan to leave late in the evening of day after tomorrow."

"Aye, sir," answered the two sailors.

"I'll keep you posted on how I'm faring," said Jim. He let the board spring back into place and replaced the bolts in their holes. When he turned from the wall, Moreau moved quietly to his side.

"Your men, they are willing?"

Jim smiled. "They're ready to leave tonight."

"Good!" exclaimed the other. "Now we look for weak spots in the wall, no?"

"Yes. And let's hope we find them!"

Together the two prisoners made an inch-by-inch inspection of the planking. Jim tested the wood at intervals with the point of the knife, taking care that he did not break the blade.

"Jim!" hissed Moreau.

Jim looked up quickly.

"Here is a place that appears decayed," said the Creole.

The midshipman watched his friend dig at the wood with his shoe buckle.

"Let me see," he said, and drove the point of his knife deeply into the wood with little pressure. Inch by inch he tested the wood toward the nearest bolt and found it spongy right up to the rusty metal. Carefully he sank

the knife point into the wood on all sides of the bolt then
dug away until he had cleared the bolthead.   He grasped
it firmly with his thumb and forefinger and tried to work
it back and forth.   Was he imagining it?—or did it give
slightly?

"I think we've found a starting point," he said cautiously, glancing over his shoulder at the door.   "You'd
better keep an eye on the passageway while I see if I can
loosen this bolt."

Moreau nodded.

"Just a minute," said Jim.   "One thing I hadn't
thought of before.   What happens to you when they
discover we're gone?"

"But this is simple, mon ami.   Before you leave, you
gag and tie me securely.   Voilà!   You have rendered me
incapable of protest or crying for help."

Jim scratched his head.   "We can't be sure that will
work."

"But why not?   I will swear to the guards that you
held me at knife point while working.   You threatened
me with instant death.   You must realize they consider you
desperate men."

"I don't know," said Jim dubiously.   "I don't want to
get you in trouble."

Moreau threw up his hands.   "Ah, bon Dieu!   Forget
your worries about others and get to work.   I go to stand
guard."

CHAPTER 12

Crisis

ON WAKING the next morning, Jim threw a hasty glance at the plank he'd worked on most of the night. He'd carefully filled the holes around the bolts with a paste of dirt and water. Unless the guards made a careful inspection they would not discover the work. From what he'd seen of their jailers this was not likely. By George! he thought, another night of uninterrupted work, and he believed he'd have enough planks loose for their escape. It was surprisingly hard work though. The old wood was sound in some places and resisted even the well-tempered knife. He hoped the blade would last.

"Eh bien. A good night's work, eh, Jim?"

Jim saw Moreau contemplating the wall from his corner of the cell.

"Aye," agreed Jim. "If the knife holds out, another night's work should see the job finished."

"You worked late, my friend. Do you feel rested?"

"I feel fine." Jim glanced at the shaft of sunlight coming through the small window. "Guess I should. It must be well along in the morning."

"It is that. But this is good. You must save your strength for the escape, too. I'm glad you are awake now. We should be having guests soon."

"Angélique?" asked Jim hopefully. He ran his fingers through his hair in an effort to straighten out the tangles.

114

Moreau smiled. "Of a certainty. Angélique is sure to come. She will know we have little food left."

"Is it possible that Visseau will come with her again? I'd like to get a final check on Barnum's arm."

"I doubt seriously if Angélique could keep him from escorting her. He is most punctilious in his attendance on the child. And after all it is through his intercession she is permitted to visit at all."

"I realize that," said Jim, but the fact of the Frenchman's constant attention stung nevertheless. He glanced sharply at Moreau. "You will not say a word of our plans to her?" he cautioned.

"You have my word," promised his cell mate.

A long hour passed and Jim began to wonder impatiently if the girl would come. Just as he was about to express his doubts he heard voices outside the door. He quickly dusted his tattered trousers.

The door swung open and for the second time Jim saw Angélique. This time, although she again ran to her father, she flashed a quick look of recognition at the midshipman.

Jim saw Visseau move into the cell and wait while the girl embraced her father. He nodded to the Frenchman and noticed he seemed unusually grave. He glanced again at Angélique and saw her eyes glisten with quick tears.

"Oh, papa!" Angélique moaned. "The worst has happened!"

"Now, now, my child." Moreau held the girl at arm's length and looked at her. "Dry those tears and tell me your troubles."

"Perhaps I had better appraise M. Moreau of the situation," Lieutenant Visseau broke in. "The military situation in the hills worsens by the hour. Dessalines has scattered the armies of Rigaud and even now the remnants of the army begin to pour into Jacmel."

Moreau nodded slowly, his face somber.

"His excellency is, of course, upset."

"He's raging like a wild beast!" Angélique put in. "He's like—like a madman!" She looked steadily at Visseau. "I think also he is mortally afraid."

Lieutenant Visseau looked embarrassed. "My position, m'sieu, is, to say the least, delicate. I must agree that the situation is confusing."

"And, papa!" cried Angélique in a stricken voice. "There is talk of—the prisoners—that is—" She stopped and turned frightened eyes on her father.

"It is their intention, my child, to eliminate the prisoners," said Moreau gently.

Angélique burst into tears.

"Now, sir," protested Lieutenant Visseau. "This is but the idle talk of a few frightened staff members. Angélique is unduly concerned. In any event, sir, nothing will happen to the political prisoners of standing such as yourself."

As if simultaneously struck by the same thought, the eyes of all three centered on Jim. He saw the sympathy in their looks.

"Oh, M. Murdock! Jim!" cried Angélique. "Why must we be the bearers of such evil tidings? Can you ever forgive us?"

"Ma'am," said Jim. "To be forewarned is to be forearmed, so to speak." He looked deeply into her eyes. "Please don't worry about us. We'll be all right."

"You are so brave, Jim," Angélique said softly.

Jim flushed. The girl's sincere respect flattered him. Looking at her lovely face he forgot Rigaud, the war, and even the United States Navy.

"Let us examine the situation further, my children," said Moreau. He looked sharply at the lieutenant. "You say Dessalines has defeated the troops of Rigaud?"

"Totally!" answered Visseau.

"What defense is being prepared for the town?"

Visseau shrugged. "Very little, I'm afraid, m'sieu. A certain confusion exists in the general staff."

"You mean they're all terrified," exclaimed Angélique, scornfully.

Visseau said, "Not all, mam'selle."

"Oh, forgive me, Pierre. Of course I didn't mean you," Angélique protested. "I don't consider you a member of that beast's staff, anyway."

Visseau shot a hasty look at the door. "Please, Angélique," he begged. "Please don't be so outspoken. These are dangerous times." He turned again to Moreau. "I have every reason to believe, m'sieu, that I can prevail on his excellency to release you before the fighting for the town begins."

Angélique stamped her foot. "It is wrong of you to give papa this hope. You know Rigaud even now prepares to run to a ship in the harbor. I can't believe he will concern himself about us."

Visseau drew himself up to his full height. "I tell you this, m'sieu. I will immediately proceed to General Rigaud and demand your release."

"That is good of you, my friend. But of more importance at the moment is to place Angélique in a place of safety."

"I assure you that I and the French gentlemen of the staff will escort your daughter to one of the French ships in the harbor."

"If you can accomplish this, my friend, you will have secured my undying gratitude," said Moreau.

Angélique set her face. "I will not go! I will not set one foot out of town unless papa is released from this vile prison."

"But, mam'selle!" implored Visseau. "You must be in a place of safety. Why, even now, with the army returning to town, there have been cases of looting. You must leave."

"Pierre is right, my dear. Jacmel under attack is no place for you. With you in safety, Pierre can do much to aid my," he shot a look at Jim and corrected himself, "*our* cause."

"I agree," said Jim firmly, "with your father and Lieutenant Visseau. You must get to a place of safety at once."

Angélique felt the concern in the midshipman's voice. She gave him a long searching look, then turned to the lieutenant. "Very well. This I will do. I will give you the rest of the day to obtain papa's release. If by tonight you have made no progress I will go to the ship and wait." She turned to her father. "After all, papa, I am in no danger in the town house during daylight."

"What do you think, Lieutenant?" asked Moreau.

The Frenchman, recognizing defeat, nodded his agreement. "Bien. I will, however, station guards at your home." He faced Jim reluctantly. "You understand, Mr. Murdock, I deplore this situation. I'm sure you understand my position."

Jim nodded. "You do all you can for Mr. Moreau and see that Angélique gets to a safe place. Don't worry about me. We Americans will make out all right."

Angélique said quickly, "Pierre, you will take a look at Mr. Murdock's sick seaman before we go, won't you?"

"But of course! It was my intention to do so. I will

leave some medicines for him. I shall return shortly," he said and walked out of the cell.

The door had no sooner closed behind the Frenchman than Angélique drew the two prisoners close. "Here, papa," she said, and thrust another knife inside his coat. "There is so little time. Pierre will get nowhere with Rigaud. That one is so frightened he doesn't know what he is doing half the time! You must try to escape—both of you!"

"Angélique—" Jim protested.

"No, no! Listen carefully! We have so little time!" she broke in. "You know an American named Hardy?"

"Why, yes," said Jim, amazed. "He's a deserter from my ship."

"No! You do not understand," Angélique protested. "He has been watching the prison and saw me leave. He found out you and papa were together and followed me in the market place. He is your friend, Jim. He told me to tell you he has a boat hidden in the swamp where it meets the bay." She fumbled at the sash about her waist. "Here," she thrust a crumpled piece of paper at the midshipman. "This will explain. He will be waiting tonight."

A great weight lifted from Jim's shoulders. Hardy no traitor after all! Many things were now clear. He knew he'd been right in placing his trust in the man. He started to speak.

"Be quiet, Jim, and listen," Angélique said impatiently, as she darted a glance toward the door. "Now here is what I plan to do. I will demand that Pierre return to the prison after dark tonight with a guard of French soldiers and a paper for your release—both of you and the two seamen. Pierre can forge Rigaud's signature."

"My child, my child," Moreau protested. "You will get the young man shot. You can't ask Pierre to risk certain death for us."

"Now, you look here, Angélique," Jim said. "You stop worrying about us and get out to that French ship just as soon as you leave here." He glanced at Moreau. "Your father and I will be all right."

"No! I will not go!"

Jim looked to Moreau for support.

"Jim is right, my child. You must not fear for our safety. We have taken precautions against such an emergency."

"I don't believe it," cried Angélique. "You're telling me this to get me to leave town. I won't go."

"All right," said Jim, exasperated. "Now you listen to me for a change. If you don't believe us, look here." He took Angélique by the arm and led her to the outer wall. Grasping the head of one of the bolts he easily slipped it from the wood. He looked down at the girl's upturned face, and smiled. "Now do you see why we're not worried, Angélique?"

"Oh, Jim. You're wonderful," she breathed. "And you'll take papa with you?"

Jim blushed under the praise. "Why, of course. You don't think we'd leave him behind, do you?"

"We?"

"I forgot to tell you," explained Jim. "We have the planks loose between this cell and the next. Barnum and Hews will go with us." He leaned closer and spoke in a low voice. "Now here's how you can help us. I have an idea that Hardy will be watching the prison if he knows you are paying us a visit. Go straight home and get your things ready for the trip out to the ship. I'm sure he will contact you in some way. Tell him about where our cell is and ask him to bring all the weapons he can lay his hands on."

"But what do I tell Pierre?" Angélique asked.

"Go ahead and demand that he try to get a release for your father, of course. Tell him your father insisted you go to the ship right away. He'll be so relieved he won't question you." He looked her straight in the eye. "The most important thing of all is for you to get out to that ship quickly."

"Jim is right, my dear. With you in safety, nothing can prevent our escape," said her father.

Angélique threw herself into her father's arms. "You will take care, won't you, papa!" she cried.

"Have no fear, my child. I am somewhat of a resourceful man myself."

At that moment the cell door swung open and Pierre Visseau walked in hurriedly. "Your man has almost completely recovered, Mr. Murdock. What stamina these seamen possess!" He turned to Moreau. "We must leave, m'sieu. Time is of the essence. You may rest assured I will do my utmost to obtain your early release." He offered his arm to Angélique. "Mam'selle, we really must hurry." He stretched out his other hand to Jim. "I have not abandoned you, sir. I will endeavor to have you released to the French. You will be assured of courteous treatment."

"Thank you, Lieutenant. And thanks for your care of Barnum. We'll never forget your kindness."

"It is nothing," said Visseau. "And now, Angélique, please. We must go."

Angélique shot a quick look at Jim, gave him a secret little smile and left with the Frenchman.

"Jim," said Moreau when the door had once again closed. "Angélique is right. Visseau will get nowhere with Rigaud. If Dessalines is within twenty miles of the town the army will be completely demoralized. That Dessalines is a tiger!" He slapped Jim on the shoulder. "But we, mon ami, do not care, eh?" He took a fencing position and whipped an imaginary rapier back and forth. "Tonight we fight our way clear!"

★

CHAPTER 13

Escape

IN SPITE of the danger of discovery, Jim couldn't wait until dark to begin working on the planks. Moreau stood by the door as lookout and Jim started to dig the wood away from the remaining bolts he'd selected for removal. With the town in such an uproar and Dessalines' army marching on the port, Jim reasoned the guards would be none too alert. Angélique's latest gift to her father had a stronger blade than the knife he'd used before. He was so anxious to get started on his own work he almost forgot about the planks Barnum and Hews were working on. Remembering, he went to the wall and sprung the plank.

"Hews," he called softly.

"Aye, sir," came the reply.

Jim passed the battered knife through the opening. "This will help you some. Now listen carefully. We'll have to work fast. Dessalines' army is marching on Jacmel. We'll have to get out of here tonight."

"We're ready any time you are, sir," said Barnum. "That French sawbones said I was as good as new."

"We don't have much more work to do, sir," said Hews. "With this knife we can dig the rest of the bolts out in no time. If it wasn't for the noise Barnum and I could probably knock 'em down right now."

"That won't be necessary," cautioned Jim. "And now

123

for the surprise of your life. We have help on the outside. Can you guess who it is?" He smiled at the blank looks on the seamen's faces. "None other than Hardy."

"Hardy!" exclaimed the two men in unison.

"That's right," explained Jim. "All that talk of his was apparently a front." He repeated what Angélique told him. "He even sent a map showing where the boat was located. He'll be watching for our escape when Miss Moreau gives him the word."

"I'm sure glad to hear that," Barnum said in relief. "I ain't hankerin' to stumble around them mountains any more. Hardy's a good man to have on your side, and if he says there's a boat hid, there'll be one."

"I'm sure there will be," agreed Jim. "Now let's get to work. One of you stand guard while the other works. We don't want the guards to find us out now."

Jim let the plank spring back into place and joined Moreau at the door.

"They'll be ready by tonight," he reported. "Now I'd better get to work myself."

"When you tire we will change places, eh?"

"Aye."

Late in the afternoon Jim paused to listen to the unmistakable rumble of cannon in the distance. He glanced at Moreau.

"I heard it, Jim," said the other. "Those guns could be fairly close. The sound would be distorted by the mountains and ravines." He cocked his head and listened again. "My guess is that the advance guard of Dessalines' army has only to fight its way through the pass above town. This should not prove difficult."

"How long do you figure we have?"

Moreau shrugged. "Who knows? Two, perhaps three hours. If any one of Rigaud's generals can persuade the army to make a stand, they could hold the pass for weeks. There is but one pass fit for an army to travel. I suspect, however, we have but little time. We must get away as soon as it is dark."

Jim glanced at the small window. "It's almost sunset now," he said. "In two hours it will be dark enough for our purpose."

"I agree," said Moreau. "We must go to the boat immediately. I can imagine the chaos in town when Dessalines overruns it."

Jim wiped the perspiration from his forehead and turned to work again. Two planks were now loose and if he could get out these last two bolts they could squeeze through. He inspected the knife. It showed signs of its rough usage but could be depended on for the rest of the job. True, it would be of little use as a weapon, but if Angélique had been able to get word to Hardy before she left for the ship, there would be weapons awaiting them.

Jim became so engrossed in his work, it was dark before he realized it.

"Jim," Moreau called softly.

Jim whirled and leaned against the wall to cover the traces of his work.

"Something is amiss, Jim. The guard has not been around with the prisoners' food."

Jim thought for a minute. Usually the guards brought each prisoner a bowl of messy stew of salt fish and manioc flour just before sunset. Not that he wanted the mess, but because the routine had been upset, he began to feel uneasy. "Do you think the guards have deserted?"

"It's possible. I can hear no one except prisoners. A better guess is that they are huddled near the gate to make a quick escape when they can."

"I don't suppose it makes much difference to us either way," said Jim. "They'll probably run and leave everyone locked in their cells."

"Yes," said Moreau, "left to the tender mercies of Dessalines. They'll be in no better position than before. He kills anyone who allows himself to be taken prisoner, if he ever gets his hands on them again."

"I guess that would discourage a soldier who thought of giving up," Jim commented. "Nice sort of war going on down here," he added drily. "Well, if the guards have left, it will make our work easier. Our only way out is through the wall, so back to work."

"Is there much more to do?"

"Another fifteen minutes will be enough, I think."

Twenty minutes later the young midshipman sat back on his heels. "That does it," he exclaimed. "Now to see how Hews and Barnum are making out."

"Jim," said the Creole. "I smell smoke."

Jim sniffed the air. "I do, too." He jumped up and caught the sill of the window and hauled himself up for a look. He could see many lights in the town but no fires. The distant crackle of muskets was quite clear. He flattened his face against the iron bars and could see lights and flares on the slopes above town. In the far distance a blaze stood out against the dark mountain. Dessalines' army had fired at least one home, he thought. They were closer than he'd expected. He dropped to the floor. No time was to be lost.

"Jim!" Moreau called urgently. "Come here quick."

Jim ran to the door.

"Down the passage! Look!"

The midshipman pressed against the small opening and looked down the passage. Against the cell doors he could see an unmistakable flickering that could only mean the prison was on fire. He whirled and faced Moreau. "We'd better get out of here, quick!"

"This place is tinder-dry, Jim. Call the others quickly!"

"Hews! Barnum!" Jim shouted. "Smash the wall down and get over here!"

Moreau ran to the outer wall and began to pull out the loose bolts. Jim joined him and together they ripped away the first plank. Behind them they could hear the seamen tearing at their wall.

By now smoke began to roll down the passageway and thin wisps fluttered into the cell.

Hews and Barnum ripped away their planks first and climbed into Jim's cell. Together the four men tore at the loosened planks on the outside wall. Although one end of each of three heavy planks had already been loosened, it took the combined efforts of all to rip them loose.

The other prisoners in the building commenced to scream in their panic; the entire prison sounded like bedlam.

Barnum turned and listened to the shouting.

"Come on!" Jim cried. "We can't help them unless we get out ourselves. Let's get these planks loose or we won't be able to help anyone," he added grimly.

The last of the planks pulled free with a ripping sound. Just as Moreau started to squeeze through the opening they heard a voice on the outside.

"Mr. Murdock!"

"That you, Hardy?" yelled Jim.

"Aye, sir. Thank heaven you're still alive!" exclaimed Hardy, with relief. "Are the others with you?"

"We're all here!"

"I've got some machetes and a musket. Can I help?"

"We're coming out now," cried Jim. "Go ahead, sir," he said to Moreau.

The Creole squeezed through, and Hews and Barnum, with many grunts, followed. It was a tight squeeze for the larger men and Jim thanked his lucky stars there'd been time to loosen enough boards. He wormed his way through after a last look at the cell.

Once outside, Jim saw Hardy handing out weapons to the other three. He slapped him on the shoulders. "Good fellow," he cried. "I hoped all along you were with us." He glanced up at the dark moonless sky. "Let's get away from this place before the fire lights up the country for miles around." Behind him he could hear the crackle of flames. "Hardy, can we help those poor devils in there?"

"We can try, sir. I saw the guards run toward town after they set the place on fire."

"Let's go, then," said Jim. He took a machete from Hardy and headed down the narrow sand strip along the prison wall. When he reached the corner of the building he glanced quickly down the road leading to town. "It seems clear, men," he shouted. "Follow me!"

The five men ran to the great double door and found it wide open. Flames leaped high above one side of the prison to give the area daylight brightness. Jim darted a look through the open door. One passageway was a burning inferno, but the other, running at right angles to it, although smoke-filled, showed no flames.

Jim ran into the prison. Fortunately, the guardroom, the first in the passageway, was not yet ablaze. He kicked open the door and began a hasty search for the keyring he'd seen the sergeant carry.

"They probably threw the keys away," yelled Moreau

through a handkerchief he held up to his face. "Maybe
we can get some of them out with this." He handed Jim
a length of heavy iron formerly used to bar the prison
gates.

Jim darted out of the guardroom and ran to the first
cell. The smoke was almost unbearable. He looked
through the hole in the door and saw the first cell was
empty. Quickly he ran to the second, Moreau and the
three sailors right behind him. That this cell was occupied was apparent; the two inmates were screaming
madly. Jim forced his bar behind the one holding the
cell door. Eager hands helped him and with a combined
heave the Americans ripped the crossbar free.

The two prisoners ran screaming out of the cell and
on down the passageway to the front door. Not even
by a wave of their hands did they indicate their thanks.

"Here's another," cried Jim and ran to the next cell.

"Look! Mr. Murdock!" screamed Barnum.

Jim whirled and stared through the swirling smoke.
Great tongues of flame were leaping into the entrance
hall from the other passageway.

"We'd better get out of here, sir!" yelled Hardy. "Or
pretty soon we won't be able to."

"One more," shouted Jim. He thrust the iron bar in
the door of the next cell and threw his whole weight into
a tremendous heave. The door flew open and two wild-
eyed prisoners lunged into the group in the passageway.
Babbling incoherently they fought off helping hands.
Jim grabbed one and faced him toward the entrance. The
man took a look and at that moment a sheet of flame
swept into the entrance. Panic-stricken, he squirmed out
of Jim's hands and ran in the opposite direction. His
cell mate, in a frenzy of fear, took off after him.

"Not that way, you fools!" screamed Jim. He started after them. A great swirling gust of acrid smoke swept down on him to send him into a spasm of coughing.

"Mr. Murdock!" cried Hardy, grabbing him by the arm. "For heaven's sake let's get out of here! You can't help them now!"

Jim turned and the five men raced toward the entrance. They fell back when a searing jet of flame roared out of the other passageway, then, when it cleared, dashed across the entranceway and through the doors.

Once clear of the prison, Jim stopped and waited for the others to gather around.

"Mr. Moreau, I guess you're better off staying with us," he said with a significant glance at the town. High above the port more fires dotted the dark side of the mountain. Even on the outskirts, where the villas of the wealthy sat cool in the shade of exotic trees, yellow tongues of flame reached for the sky. "Looks like Dessalines' troops will soon take over."

M. Moreau drew his forearm across a blackened and singed brow. He brought the machete to a sword salute and said, "You are the captain, M. Murdock. Lead, I will follow."

Jim turned to Hardy. "Where's the boat?"

Hardy pointed toward the marsh. "I've got her hid in the cove on the sea side of the swamp, sir. It's not more'n a couple of feet deep where the marsh joins the bay. We can wade over without any trouble."

Jim glanced back at the burning prison, now an inferno of flame and black smoke. Nothing more could be done here. He had the men under him to think of. If the deliberate firing of the prison was any sample of the army's actions, he'd better get his group clear as quickly as possible. It would be good to get afloat again. He

looked around the small party. Hardy's face was black
with soot. His shirt, wet with perspiration, clung to his
body as if molded there. Hews, an iron bar in his hands,
stared at the blazing prison with bloodshot eyes, as if
unable to credit their good fortune in escaping. Barnum
massaged his wounded arm and fixed his eyes on the marsh
they were to skirt, while Moreau, his fine clothes scorched
and torn, held himself erect and poised as ever.

The night breeze seemed to have strengthened and Jim
hoped it was not all due to the tremendous updraft caused
by the prison fire.

Hardy, in the lead, pointed to a great pile of sand at
a point where the edge of the marsh ran down to the bay.
"Gun emplacement," he said. "Been deserted for the
past couple of days. Reckon Rigaud needed every man
he could get for the army in the hills." He stepped forward briskly.

Close by the temporary embankment, hastily piled up
to provide a gun mount, Hardy stopped and looked
around carefully.

"Miss Angélique," he called.

Jim and Moreau stared at him in amazement.

"What did you say?" Jim cried.

Hardy ran to the top of the embankment and called
down into the depression housing an old carriage gun.
"Miss Angélique!" he called in a louder voice.

Jim scrambled up the bank and grabbed Hardy by the
arm. He swung the sailor around roughly. "Why are
you calling Miss Moreau, Hardy? She's out in the harbor
on one of the French ships!"

Moreau ran up, his face chalk-white. "Was my daughter to meet us here?" he demanded. "Speak, man! Where
is she?"

Hardy stared helplessly at the two men. "When she

told me you planned to escape tonight, she said she'd meet us here at the gun. She was going to bring food and guns. I thought that was part of the plan." He shook his head slowly. "She didn't say anything about a French ship, sir." His stricken eyes implored Jim to believe him.

Jim turned and stared toward the town. Fires had reached the homes close in. Even at this distance he could see toylike figures running around in the light of the flames on the slope. He exchanged looks with Moreau, then ran down the sandbank, Hardy and the Creole after him.

"You men go on to the boat," he ordered. "Mr. Moreau and I will go into town to make sure the young lady is safe."

He hoped his voice was steady, but he could feel his heart pounding with apprehension. If Angélique said she would meet them with food and guns, nothing short of disaster would keep her away, unless . . . He swung on Moreau.

"I'm sure Visseau forced her to go to the ship for her own safety, sir. We'll check to make sure."

Moreau nodded grimly and headed down the road for town.

Jim started after him and called back over his shoulder. "Don't wait more than a couple of hours for us. Shove off if the troops get near the boat!" He raced after the Creole with only a quick glance to see if the sailors were carrying out his orders. To his amazement he saw all three sailors pounding after him. He slowed a little to let them catch up.

"We figure you might need a little help, Mr. Murdock," panted Hews. He shot a doubtful look at the midshipman's grim face. "There really ain't time to argue with us, sir."

★

CHAPTER 14

Jacmel

B Y THE TIME Moreau, in the lead, reached the houses on the edge of town, he had slowed his pace to a steady trot. The determined party began to pass terrified refugees fleeing the town with such worldly goods as they could keep on carts and carriages. All of them, to whom the very name Dessalines meant death, raced by in panic. Few, if any, gave more than a quick glance to Jim's group. Even fewer would have recognized the blackened, perspiring sailors as Americans. Among the escaping refugees, Jim recognized a few soldiers in their tattered uniforms. The defenses must be crumbling, he thought, if the officers couldn't keep their men in town.

Just a block from the plaza, Jim caught his first sight of looters. They were under the loose leadership of a soldier who directed their efforts to break down the door of a large home. Jim's knuckles whitened as he gripped the weapon in his hand; glancing down he was surprised to see he still clutched the iron bar he'd picked up at the prison. When the five men reached the next corner, Moreau stopped and stared at the milling mass of humanity in the plaza. On the bay side, terrified crowds of men, women, and children fought their way toward the quay. There, badly overloaded small boats of every description ferried the townspeople to the ships in the harbor.

On the other side of the great square, a troop of

cavalry, the points of their long lances flashing, rode down a confused mob of soldiers trying to fight their way to the harbor. The noise, a swelling roar of screams and curses, beat on the young midshipman's ears.

"Where is your house?" he yelled.

Moreau, not trusting his voice, pointed toward the street where the cavalry vainly tried to beat the soldiers back to the town's defenses. He swung his arm a little to the left and in a hoarse, gasping voice shouted one word: "Alley!"

He started out, stumbled and almost fell, but recovered and doggedly took up a trot toward a dark gaping entrance between two large buildings.

Jim realized their strength lay in their ability to act as a single co-ordinated unit. A quick glance assured him the three sailors were close on his heels. Up ahead, he saw they must pass through the fringe of a milling group of frightened soldiers desperately trying to avoid the long lances of the cavalry. He saw one soldier, pursued by a trooper, drop his cumbersome musket in an attempt to escape. He watched the point of the long lance steady, then enter the man's back just between his shoulder blades. For a few yards the momentum of the horse and rider carried the impaled soldier along the street, his arms and legs sprawled grotesquely. Jim watched the trooper jerk his mount to a savage halt, yank the lance free and look around for his next victim.

Jim was not the only witness to the cold-blooded murder. A group of frightened soldiers, hugging the wall of a large building on the corner, fled in a body when they saw the trooper free his lance.

It was obvious the soldiers were heading for the darkness of the alley. Jim realized his own party would have a difficult time forcing its way through the leaderless throng in the narrow alley. He put on speed and passed Moreau, still in the lead.

"Close up," he called over his shoulder. "We'll have to force our way through."

The three sailors, realizing his intent, immediately moved up to form a flying wedge.

Jim grasped the iron bar in both hands and held it chest-high before him. The first of the fleeing soldiers reached the end of the alley and turned, uncertainly. Crazed with fear, they nevertheless understood the alley could offer but temporary safety. The quay and safety of the small boats lay in the opposite direction.

The soldiers' momentary indecision was all Jim needed. He drove forward, felt his iron bar thud into the chest of a soldier to send him reeling. Hands tore at his arms as he tried desperately to get swinging room for his crude weapon. He heard Hardy grunt and saw him hoist a man high and throw him into a group making a concerted rush.

Suddenly, one of the soldiers, his eyes wide with fear, screamed and pointed. Jim risked a quick look over his shoulder. A trooper, his lance leveled, was bearing down on the unsuspecting sailors! There was no time to cry a warning. His back toward the plaza, Hews presented a perfect target for the lowered lance. With a strangled yell Jim hurled himself at the lance point, swinging his iron bar at the same time.

Hews turned his head in time to see the deflected point flash past his shoulder. Catlike, he whirled and grasped the shaft with both hands. He gave a tremendous heave and almost dragged the trooper from his saddle. Frightened now, the trooper released the lance and jerked savagely on the reins to swing his mount clear of the melee.

Jim felt the pressure of the soldiers' attack on his own group diminish as the maddened men centered their efforts on the horse and rider. He saw one soldier reach for the mounted man to drag him from his horse. The trooper drew his pistol and fired pointblank into his attacker's face.

But there was no stopping the enraged deserters. They surrounded the horse, and those who still had knives and machetes began to hack at the horse's legs. The poor beast went down screaming in anguish. Jim saw the white-clad trooper disappear into a sea of grasping hands and flashing blades. He grabbed Moreau by the arm. "Let's get out of here!" he yelled, and dragged him into the alley. "Where's the house?"

"The garden borders on this alley, Jim. We can get in through the back entrance."

Jim looked around. The three sailors had pulled clear of the fighting mob and now joined him. "We go straight up this alley," he cried. "Keep close and don't stop for anything! Lead the way, sir," he shouted to Moreau.

The Creole ran up the alley, followed by the four Americans. Even in the darkness Jim could make out furtive figures hugging the walls and doorways. Though the tumult of the plaza diminished as they got further away, the terrified screams of women and children still rang in his ears. Up ahead, the flames now shot their fiery tongues high above the houses. Not much further, he prayed silently, or we'll find Moreau's house in flames, too. Though he tried to tell himself Angélique was safe aboard ship, a cold fear gnawed at his chest.

They ran past a high wall on their right. About midway along its length, Moreau turned and raced to a small door recessed into the stone. He shook it with all his waning strength. "Locked!" he gasped.

"Here, let me!" Jim threw his weight against the solid door with a jolt that almost shook his teeth loose. He swung around, his eyes searching wildly for a ram. Their machetes, even the heavy iron in his hand, would be useless against the solid door.

Hardy shouted and dashed across the alley. He wrapped his hands around a metal hitching post embedded in a block of stone and heaved. The others rushed to his side, and together they pulled stone and all from the ground. Holding it level with their waists like a battering-ram, all five men drove forward at Jim's "Now!"

The wood shattered under the smashing blow, and Moreau leaped through the opening with a joyful shout, followed by the others.

Once through the door, the Creole led them through a garden of exquisite loveliness. Jim threw a quick look at the shuttered windows of the house before them. He could see no lights or signs of life.

Moreau ran across the flat stones of a small terrace and threw his body against the double doors leading into the house. Jim joined him, and together they hit the wood with their shoulders. The door flew open so suddenly both men went down.

"Look out!" Barnum cried behind Jim.

The midshipman looked up to see at least a dozen looters in the candlelit room. To Jim's surprise they appeared to be seamen. They stared in astonishment at the blackened and bloodstained group at the terrace door. One man, holding a burlap bag filled with silver, shot a frightened look at the Americans and scurried out the front door. Others, braver or more greedy, moved closer together and waited, their naked machetes shining in the yellow candlelight.

The antagonists eyed each other cautiously. Bolder

now that they saw but five men in the attacking party, the looters started a menacing approach.

A heavy table in the middle of the room caught Jim's eye. "The table," he muttered. "We'll pick it up and rush 'em."

"Aye," growled Barnum. "While they're bunched up, we can hit 'em all at once."

"Let's go!" yelled Jim and led a rush across the room.

The looters, surprised by the suddenness of the attack, recoiled momentarily.

Jim and his party scooped up the table on the run and drove straight at the confused enemy, most of whom went down under the impact of the heavy wood shield. Those still on their feet headed for the front door.

The three American sailors started after the fleeing enemy but after one look at the street outside hastily shut and barred the door.

"Looks like the whole army's outside fightin' in the street," Hews panted.

Jim realized they had little time left. Soon Moreau's house would be in Dessalines' hands. Out of the corner of his eye, he saw Moreau bound up the steps of a wide stairway.

"Disarm those men!" he shouted. He headed for the stairs.

At the top of the stairs Jim paused. At one end of the second floor hall he saw Moreau kick open a door, raise his machete and start in.

"Papa! Watch out!"

Jim heard Angélique's scream of terror.

The midshipman raced down the hall and burst into the room. On the far side of the room he saw Angélique, back against a wall and a heavy vase in her hand. At his feet, Moreau was on his hands and knees shaking his head as if dazed.

"Look out, Jim!" screamed Angélique and threw the vase with all her strength. Jim heard the sharp crack of a pistol and felt the breeze of a ball as it shaved his head. He crouched and whirled to face his enemy. In the corner, an empty pistol in his hand, his face contorted with rage, stood Antoine Cruet.

"Thees time, Murdock, you die for sure," the pirate growled, drawing his cutlass and advancing confidently on the midshipman, armed only with an iron bar.

Jim sized up his enemy. Cruet handled the cutlass like an old hand with this particular weapon. He knew he must outwit his opponent.

Cruet lunged forward, the point of the cutlass leaping out with the speed of a snake's tongue. Jim parried the blade with a quick shift of his bar; then ducked as Cruet aimed a whistling blow at his head.

I'll have to be careful, thought Jim. The man's quick as a cat, and there's a great deal of strength in that wiry figure. He gave ground warily, trying to draw the pirate to the center of the room. He saw Cruet's eyes flick toward the door and heard Moreau move up behind him.

"Keep clear, sir!" Jim ordered. "He's mine!"

Moreau backed away and moved quickly to his daughter's side to put a protecting arm around her. The two of them stared at the duel in the center of the room.

Jim saw beads of perspiration gather on the pirate's forehead. Cruet, he figured, was wondering how the two of them got into the house with his seamen stationed downstairs.

"Your crew took to their heels like the rats they are," Jim taunted.

Cruet, realizing his plight, wasted no words in answering. He lunged forward, slashing and cutting with the heavy cutlass until Jim was hard-pressed to counter the raining blows. He gave ground slowly. The exertions of the evening had taken more of his strength than he realized. He could not keep up this defense much longer. His breath came in short gasps. Cruet followed up his advantage and continued to thrust and cut.

Jim's right arm began to hurt like fire. Tiny needle thrusts in the forearm warned him he could not continue much longer. He knew he must drive home a slashing attack while he still had enough strength left.

Cruet, in his eagerness to end the unequal battle, lunged forward with a sweeping blow. For a fraction of a second it left him off balance. Jim sensed his opportunity and reacted quickly. He swung the iron in a wild blow at the pirate's head. Cruet parried in time, but the heavy iron smashing on his cutlass blade almost paralyzed his arm. His benumbed fingers lost their grip; the cutlass dropped to the floor.

Cruet's eyes darted around the room. Like a cornered rat, he searched for a way out as he backed away from the midshipman. Passing close to a chest of drawers, he swept the top clear with a motion that rained bottles on Jim. He darted for a window, kicked the shutters open, jumped to the window ledge and dropped out of sight.

Jim ran across the room and looked out the window. A few feet below the sill he saw a figure poised on a small roof in the flickering light of the fires. A second later it was gone.

Jim turned slowly to face the Moreaus.

"Oh, Jim!" cried Angélique. "You were magnifique!"

"He got away," muttered the midshipman, and drew his hand across his forehead.

"It does not matter, Jim," said Moreau. "Come, we must leave at once."

"Aye," Jim agreed. He moved to the center of the room and looked around. "Where can we see the street?"

"Follow me," cried Angélique and crossed the hall to enter a bedroom. She threw open the shutters and drew back hastily.

Jim moved up behind her and looked down. The noise of battle was deafening. In the glare of the fires he saw a dozen horses surrounded by a body of troops massing for an attack. The squat figure on a white horse seemed familiar. The mount wheeled and Jim looked down at Dessalines. The general's hoarse croaking voice kept shouting, "Kill! Kill! Kill!"

Occasionally, during his imprisonment, Jim had thought they might find safety with Toussaint's greatest general. Now, as he stared at that hate-filled face, he realized there could be no safety for the Americans with that army. The very fact that he had befriended the Moreaus was his death warrant. Dessalines meant to kill every inhabitant of Jacmel.

Jim backed away from the window. He grabbed Angélique by the arm and pulled her toward the door. "Hurry! We'll go out through the garden!"

★

CHAPTER 15

A Great Loss

FEW IF ANY of the surviving inhabitants of Jacmel would ever be able to erase the memory of that terror-filled night. Jim knew that he never could. Rigaud's mounted troops were apparently unable to stem the disgraceful flight of his foot soldiers. When Jim and his small group ran into the garden, he began to think escape was hopeless. The fighting seemed to be completely around them. Flaming chunks of wood rained down on the whole town, and it was only a matter of minutes before Moreau's house would go up in flames too.

Jim dashed across the garden and made a quick inspection of the alley. So far it looked clear. He paused only long enough to make sure his party was intact. He saw Hardy throw away his machete, grasp a three-foot chain hanging from the shattered garden gate and tear it loose.

"This'll serve better'n any machete," he growled.

Jim nodded approval and led the group into the alley. Well-lighted now that the fires were so close, the alley would provide no cover. He realized they would have difficulty in trying to set too fast a pace; Angélique would have trouble keeping up. After a minute or two he was pleasantly surprised, however, to see the girl running with an easy swing and holding her own.

Nearing the plaza again, the midshipman saw the situation was even more hopelessly confused than before. The

142

entrance of the alley was completely blocked. Jim stopped.

"This is hopeless," he panted. "We'll never get through there again."

Angélique darted a look at the building on their right. "Papa!" she cried. "It is the home of Thérèse the dressmaker. Come," she said urgently to Jim. "I know the house well. We can get through to the next street." She pointed to a closed door on the alley level.

Jim ran to the door, kicked it open and looked in. The odor of charred wood was strong, but he could see no flames within.

Angélique pushed past him, impatiently. "Come, Jim. I will lead you through." She disappeared into the house.

Jim followed, and although the interior was lighted only by the flickering flames outside, enough light filtered through the windows to enable him to make out the girl running down a central hall. He raced after her, the others close on his heels.

Very quickly they reached the front of the house. Angélique threw the front door open and would have rushed into the street had not Jim caught her by the arm.

"Hold," he said. "Let's take a look out there, first." He pulled her back into the room and moved cautiously to the door.

The street was strangely quiet after the confusion of the other thoroughfares. Keeping well in the shadows, he made a quick survey. About fifty yards up the street from the door, he saw a small fieldpiece with perhaps twenty soldiers around it.

The others moved up behind him and peered over his shoulder.

"They'll never let us by without a fight," muttered Hews.

"We can't go back," said Hardy.

Jim heard the chain rattle in his grasp.

The midshipman thought quickly. They were both right. The soldiers would run them down if they tried to make a break toward the plaza. He eyed the group of soldiers in the street. They were probably frightened half to death anyway, knowing they were about to face Dessalines' veteran army. Maybe bold action was needed. If he led his sailors in a quick surprise feint at their rear, when they expected the enemy from the other direction, he might scatter them long enough for Moreau to get his daughter clear.

"Jim." Moreau plucked at the midshipman's elbow. "The house across the street." He pointed to a large home almost directly opposite their hiding place. "It is the home of a good friend. If we can get to it, we can pass through and put more distance between us and the mob. That is also the direction of the swamp."

Jim glanced across the street and noticed the front door had been knocked in. He swung around and grabbed the Creole by the shoulder. "We'll make a run for it," he said. "If they rush us while we cross, don't stop for anything. Get Angélique in that door. We'll hold them off until you do." He looked at the sailors. "Ready?" he asked.

"But, Jim, I should be helping—"

"You get Angélique into the house. The rest of us will hold back the soldiers. Keep your eye on that door and don't let anything stop you." He pulled Angélique up beside him. "Come!" he ordered in a low voice, and moved quickly into the street.

Jim ignored the roar of the crowd in the plaza, far down the street to his left, and kept a wary eye on the soldiers around the small cannon. Beyond the gun he

could see fires roaring out of control up the street, and
he realized that the soldiers would soon have to retreat
without facing the enemy at this spot.

The group had reached the middle of the street before
a soldier shouted and pointed in their direction. Jim
gave Angélique a push toward the door and swerved to
meet the attack. He saw about a dozen soldiers running
toward him. Raising his cutlass, he headed for the fore-
most of the attackers. Hardy raced ahead of him, the
heavy iron chain whistling in great circles above his head.

Jim heard a sickening crunch when the chain caught
the leader flush in the head. Before the soldiers could
back clear, two more crumpled under the impact of the
wildly swinging chain. Jim moved in, his cutlass flashing.
Hews' lance jabbed at the soldiers. Unable to cope with
the sudden and unorthodox attack, the soldiers broke and
ran.

"Quick!" yelled Jim. "Back to the door."

All four Americans raced for the doorway and the
safety of the darkness.

Moreau, assured that all were back, cried, "This way,
Jim!" and headed toward the rear of the house. He led
them through a garden similar to his own and on into
another alley.

"We'll have to move quickly toward the bay now, Jim,
or we will never get to the boat," said Moreau.

Jim's stinging eyes flicked up and down the alley.
"We'll take the lead now. You and Angélique keep right
behind us."

Acrid smoke swirled down the alley to send the entire
group into a fit of coughing. The wind was rising. The
great fires in town were drawing air into the vortex of
the hot flames.

When they reached the end of the alley, Jim was dis-

mayed to find it thronged with panic-stricken refugees
headed away from the plaza. For a moment the direction
of their flight confused him, then he understood the
reason for it. Unable to find room in the boats, they too
were seeking a hiding place in the swamp. What if they
passed beyond and discovered the boat? Bunching his
shoulders, the midshipman leaped forward into the stream
of refugees.

"Keep together!" he cried, and rammed his way to the
center of the street.

The frightened townspeople cleared a path for the
five bloody and dirt-streaked men and the girl. The
Americans, unused to the brutality in the war-torn island,
steeled themselves against the heart-rending scenes around
them. Helpless old ones, knocked to the ground by those
younger and stronger, were trampled underfoot. Children crushed beneath the wheels of heavily loaded carts;
screaming mothers; rearing horses, their eyes white with
fear: all were a part of the terrible tableau. Deserters
from the army robbed the weak, even as they too sought
to escape. On more than one occasion he saw groups of
these vultures attack unarmed civilians. Jim regretted he
could not assist the weak, but he knew they must move
fast. His responsibility was to his own party.

Not until he was well clear of the town did Jim stop
and look back. The whole of Jacmel seemed ablaze.
Fortunately, almost all of the refugees were near the upper
reaches of the swamp, trying to find safety in the patches
of canebrake. A few slunk by now, but all of them gave
Jim's party a wide berth.

The roaring flames of the burning port lighted up the
mountainside and bay alike. The bay was alive with
small boats. One more, thought Jim, would certainly
not be questioned. He turned to the road ahead. A dark

heap of smoldering wood and small fires was all that remained of the prison. He shuddered, thinking of the
trapped prisoners and the fate that might have been his
own. Shrugging off his thoughts, he glanced over his
little group. The three sailors, blackened and singed,
looked more vicious than any pirates he'd ever seen.
Moreau, his slender body erect, studied the burning town
with a passive face. What his thoughts might be, Jim
could not guess. Angélique, her mouth half-open in sheer
astonishment at the spectacle, looked even more lovely
than ever as she stood surrounded by the battered men.

"We'd better go on, sir," Jim said quietly to Moreau.

The Creole seemed to shake himself out of his reverie
and turned quickly. "But of course, my boy. We are
not out of danger yet, no?"

"And you, Angélique?" asked Jim. "Are you ready to
go on?"

The girl turned grateful eyes on the young midshipman. "I am ready whenever you are, Jim," she answered
with a tired smile. "I will not hold you back."

"You haven't so far, ma'am. That's a fact," said Hews
admiringly.

"Let's push on then," said Jim. "The longer we leave
that boat, the more chance it gives some deserters to find
it." He turned on Hardy. "Did you hide it pretty well?"

"I pulled it back into the swamp, sir. I figgered it was
well-hidden. 'Course I didn't know that half the army
would be scattered around the bay."

"It'll probably still be there," Jim said. "Let's go and
get it."

The small group headed on down the prison road,
passed the smoldering prison, and stopped again in front
of the abandoned gun emplacement at the edge of the
swamp.

Jim stared down the edge of the swamp grass where it touched the bay.

"Hardy, you've been along this stretch before. What's the depth of the water?"

"No more'n knee-high, most of the way," answered the sailor. "Couple of places," he cast a covert glance at Angélique, "water might be well over your knees. Nowhere is it really deep, though."

"Firm bottom?"

"Aye, sir. Sand and shells. Good walkin' all the way."

"You take the lead," ordered Jim. "We'll follow."

The group hadn't covered more than fifty feet before Jim realized Angélique was having a difficult time of it. Her voluminous skirt, wet to well above her knees, impeded her every step. She struggled on without a word, but the midshipman could hear her labored breath as she tried to keep up. He slipped the cutlass through his wide leather belt and moved up behind her. "Here, Angélique, let me help you," he said, and picked her up in his arms. He heard her gasp in surprise, grow rigid, then slowly relax. Her arm slipped around his neck.

"I am not too heavy, Jim?" she murmured in his ear.

"Holy Moses, no!" the midshipman replied emphatically and wondered if she sensed he was blushing.

Halfway across the swamp's edge, Hardy, in the lead, stopped so suddenly the others bumped together in confusion.

"What's the trouble?" demanded Jim.

"Look up there!"

The midshipman stared ahead. He could see where the swamp ended; could see a firm white sand beach stretching on around the bay. As his eyes followed the beach line, he caught a flickering of light among the trees behind the sand.

"We have company," said Hardy.

"Perhaps they are refugees like ourselves," said Moreau.

"Perhaps," answered Hardy and met Jim's eyes. Each knew what was in the other's mind: Refugees would not dare show lights so openly.

"Make as little noise as possible," ordered Jim. "I think they're too far away to cause us any trouble. We can find the boat and get away without their seeing us."

Hardy moved on cautiously, hugging the edge of the swamp. Slowly he closed the distance to the sand beach ahead, until, at a point some twenty feet from firm ground, he parted the rushes and disappeared into the swamp.

The others heard a startled exclamation, watched Hardy burst out of the tall grass, a surprised expression on his face.

"It's gone," he cried.

"Are you sure this is the right place?" asked Jim anxiously.

"Aye," growled Hardy. "I reckon them people up the beach found it." He glared at the flickering fires ahead.

"We'd better see," said Jim quietly.

With utmost caution the little party waded on to the beach. Jim put Angélique down.

"Thank you, Jim," she said demurely. "I was not too heavy?"

"Not at all," lied Jim gallantly, trying not to show how badly winded he was.

"Do we go get 'em, sir?" asked Hews, still clutching the lance he had torn from the trooper's hands.

"We take a look anyway," answered the midshipman. "Follow me and keep close to the trees. They won't be able to spot us here in the shadows." He motioned the girl to the rear. "Angélique, you keep well behind us and out of sight."

Jim moved from shadow to shadow, gradually closing the distance to the lights. The loss of their boat could prove fatal. Without some sort of craft to clear the island before daylight, their chances of escaping one army or the other were very slim.

★

CHAPTER 16

Angélique Has a Plan

BEFORE Jim had covered a hundred yards he felt a tap on his shoulder. "Look out there, sir." Hardy pointed down the beach. "That's the boat I hid." Jim studied the small fishing craft riding low in the water at anchor a few yards off the beach. It lay close to the spot where he'd seen the lights earlier. He could see no one in or around it. That didn't seem right. Anyone in his right mind would keep a close watch on his boat this night. He turned to the others in his party.

"Wait here in the shadows. I'll sneak up there and have a look."

"You want me to go with you, sir?" asked Hews.

"You stay here and take charge," Jim ordered the gunner's mate. "I'll be back shortly." He slipped into the dark shadows of the palm grove.

The closer to the lights he got, the louder became the sounds of revelry. Jim could hear shouting and cursing; whoever they were, they seemed confident of their strength. He moved cautiously now, running lightly from tree to tree each time he saw the way clear. Very shortly he found himself near the edge of a small clearing. He dropped to his hands and knees and crawled forward to a small bush. Parting the leaves for a look, he saw a group of soldiers around a fire. Some lay sprawled drunkenly on the sand, and others staggered about, waving bottles wildly. Whatever the cause for celebration, Jim mused, they were certainly going at it whole hog. If there was no one in the boat, he shouldn't have too much trouble getting it back. He ducked back away from the bush and crawled to the beach.

Not fifty yards away, riding low but easily on the calm surface, the boat swung to her anchor. Evidently the tide paralleled the beach at this point, because he got a broadside view of the trim craft. If he could get out there unobserved and cut the anchor line, the tide would carry the boat down toward his own party. He wished mightily the burning town across the bay didn't light everything up so much; however, he knew he had to risk a try at recovering their transportation.

With a wary eye on the clearing, he crept across the sand and into the bay. He felt better when the shallow water covered him completely, as he knew he'd be more difficult to see. Careful not to cause any ripples, he moved slowly but surely toward the boat. He found the water only waist-deep at the anchor. Easing the machete out of his belt, he kept the bright blade under water and cut the anchor rope. He watched the boat drift slowly away. Pausing only long enough for a quick glance at the unsuspecting soldiers around the fire, he let the tide carry him along, too.

When well clear of the lights, Jim grasped the stern and started to hoist himself over the side. Just as his head cleared the stern he found himself face to face with a soldier! Startled, his first thought was to push clear, when it dawned on him that the man's eyes were closed, his mouth half-open. Asleep or drunk, Jim thought, and as his eye caught sight of an empty bottle beside the man's hand, he felt much better. Let him sleep until they were

far enough away so that a yell wouldn't bring help. He
eased back into the water and drifted along calmly with
the tide.

Well down the beach, Jim eased the boat closer inshore. If Hews and the others were watching, they would
realize he had recovered their means of escape. Finally
he saw all five of his party break out of the palm grove
and run across the beach.

Jim stood up in the waist-deep water, held the boat
steady; then reached over the gunwale to wrap a muscular
arm around the soldier's neck. The man awoke with a
strangled gasp and commenced to kick wildly.

"Here, give me a hand," Jim said to Hews and Hardy
as they splashed toward him. "Tie him up and gag him;
then haul him back into the bush." He removed two
pistols from the soldier's belt.

Barnum looked into the boat. "They sure loaded
this boat down, Mr. Murdock," he exclaimed.

Jim glanced at a pile of jute bags stowed in the bottom.
No wonder the boat rode so low in the water. He hauled
one toward him and realized it contained loot from the
town.

"Most of these heavy bags will have to come out," he
announced. "This boat would swamp in any sea at all."
He reached over and commenced to toss the bags over the
side.

The others joined him in his work, and, when a goodly
number had been removed, Barnum looked up at the
young officer. He held a bag in his hand, and, as he
shifted it, Jim could hear the unmistakable clink of silver.

"Couldn't we carry just a few?" the sailor asked. "Just
for ballast, sir?"

Jim noticed the others waiting for his answer. He

smiled. "Aye! 'Tis lawful prize. Stow the rest along the keel."

Away from the whirling winds nearer to the raging fires, there was but a scant breeze. Jim decided not to set the sail. The boat would be less conspicuous if they paddled. He detailed Hardy and Hews each to a paddle and took the tiller. Slowly the boat gained steerageway, under the powerful strokes of the two sailors, and moved away from the shore. He took time to look around the bay. Although many of the refugee-laden craft had cleared the port, quite a few remained. He scanned the harbor and saw no more small boats leaving the quay. No doubt Dessalines' army had gained the plaza.

A hundred yards off the beach he changed course with a slight pressure on the tiller. It wouldn't do to get among the larger ships still at anchor. He did not want to risk capture by any ships still loyal to Rigaud, or for that matter by the French, either. It was only necessary to skirt the beach until clear of the harbor. Once in the open sea, they could search for American or neutral shipping.

The way seemed clear ahead, except for a brig anchored close inshore and Jim felt they could slip by it easily. He eased the boat nearer the beach. There were still a great number of small craft milling around among the larger ships, evidently townspeople looking for passage.

Suddenly a piercing scream rang out. Jim saw Moreau point and watched a half-dozen men swarm out of a long-boat into a fishing craft. He saw knives flash and heard a shot.

"Looks like some of the refugees are losing their belongings," commented Hews, casually.

"The greed of mankind is beyond comprehension," said Moreau, sadly.

Jim felt Angélique's eyes on him. He looked across the water to the two boats not more than a cable's length away, then faced the girl. "I'd like to help them but there's little we can do. If we get out there among those boats either you or we Americans might be recognized."

"I know, Jim," agreed Angélique. "However, it does seem to me a pity those fiends cannot be punished."

"Sir!"

Jim looked quickly at the bow where Barnum stood pointing toward the brig.

"Ain't that the *Rover?*"

Jim studied the brig, carefully.

"It looks like her."

Hardy paused in his stroke; he raised his paddle clear of the water and stared at the ship. "That's her all right, Mr. Murdock," he said. "Cruet had a crew bring her around a couple days ago. Admiral Cruet," he stressed the title, contemptuously, "figgered to use her as his flagship. I'd 'a' told you sooner, but it slipped my mind."

Jim stared thoughtfully at the trim brig. His first command! Just the sight of her brought back a flood of memories. How proud he'd been when he cleared the side of the *Victory.* Captain of his own ship! How handsomely the brig had responded to rudder and canvas. And then he remembered his captain screaming at him from the deck of the *Victory,* and the *Rover's* broadside smashing into the American ship.

The midshipman saw the three sailors glancing from time to time at the brig. He caught Hews looking at him covertly. He knew the men sympathized with him, and the knowledge stung. Try as he might, he could not keep his eyes off the ship. The course he'd set would take them fairly close. As the distance narrowed, he was puzzled by the lack of activity aboard. He studied the ship. A white light on the bow and another on the stern were the only ones visible. There were no more than a half-dozen men topside, and these were gathered aft at the stern, watching the town burn.

"Ain't much of a crew aboard, seems like," said Barnum from the bow.

Jim made no reply. He saw Hews and Hardy pause in their stroke, dart a quick look at him, then resume their paddling.

"This ship, Jim," said Moreau quietly. "She is the command you lost to Cruet, yes?"

Jim nodded.

Moreau stared at the brig, then faced Jim.

"I think perhaps Barnum is right. There are but a handful of men aboard."

Jim could feel the sailors' eyes on him. "That may be," he said stiffly, and turned his eyes away to stare ahead.

"Would you not try to take your ship back again, Jim?" asked Moreau. "I for one would be pleased to assist."

The two sailors made no pretense of paddling now. They sat, paddles poised, waiting for their officer's next words.

Jim looked at his men, avoided Angélique's eyes and said, "Too dangerous."

"But, Jim, these are but small odds compared—" Moreau began a protest.

"I know, papa," interrupted Angélique, "why he will not do it. He is afraid for me." She faced Jim with pleading eyes. "Jim, put me ashore until you have captured your ship. Please, Jim!" she begged.

"No," said Jim, "we've been lucky so far. It's too much of a chance."

"If I were not here you would try!" Angélique, her eyes flashing, suddenly stood up. "Very well. I will jump in the water and you will not have me to worry about."

The boat gave a sudden lurch as the girl put one foot on the gunwale.

Jim grabbed for her, caught her arm and dragged her back to the seat. "Angélique!" he growled. "For heaven's sake, behave yourself! Sit down and be quiet."

"I will not be quiet." She struggled in his arms, then suddenly stopped fighting him. "Besides, I have thought of a plan."

Moreau watched his daughter's face carefully. He looked at Jim. "I think perhaps you should listen, my friend; the child has a head on her shoulders."

Without waiting for the midshipman's approval, Angélique unfolded her plan.

"All of the men are at one end of the ship," she explained. "Papa and I will let you and your brave men," she swept the admiring sailors with a warm smile, "off at the other end. Then papa and I will take the boat to the opposite end and beg to be taken aboard."

"But—" protested Jim.

"Oh! they will let us aboard, Jim." Angélique reached down and touched a jute bag. "When I hold up one of these, and they hear the sound of silver, they will pay attention."

The three sailors leaned forward, their faces wreathed in smiles.

"While papa and I engage them in conversation, voilà! You capture them from behind." She threw up her hands in glee. "Is it not a good plan, yes?"

Jim heard the three sailors murmur their approval and saw them nod in agreement. He studied the brig for a long minute: her deck, her rigging, and the men aft.

"It's a fine plan," he agreed. "But—"

Angélique grabbed the gunwale and started to stand up.

"No—wait! Angélique!" he protested. When she sat down again, he looked at her steadily. "All right," he said. "We'll do it." He held her by the wrist. "We'll do it," he repeated, "but no more of your nonsense. I want you to listen to me carefully and do exactly as I say!"

"Aye, aye, Mr. Murdock," said Angélique meekly.

The fishing boat drifted silently down on the anchor chain of the brig. By keeping the ship between their own craft and the burning town Jim had been able to approach in comparative darkness. He motioned to Barnum, in the bow, who grabbed the anchor chain and held on to let the stern of the fishing boat swing with the tide, in under the brig's sharp bow.

The midshipman pulled Moreau and his daughter close. "When we get up on the bow," he whispered, "I'll give you a little push. The tide'll carry you aft." He shot an anxious look at the girl. "Be very careful. Keep them talking if you can. They will want to get the loot aboard first, so hand it up to them one bag at a time. Stay in the boat. We should have them before they can take many aboard."

Silently the sailors hauled themselves up over the bowsprit. Jim gave a last look around the fishing boat. He turned to Angélique and put a pistol in her hand. "In case any of them get too close," he said.

As Jim swung clear he gave the boat a slight push with

his feet. He watched the tide take charge, saw the boat slew around and start to drift down the brig's side. Hauling himself on deck he saw his three men huddled behind the capstan. "Wait till they see the boat," he cautioned the eager seamen.

Down the deck Jim saw the men aft turn, draw their weapons and run to the quarter rail. One of them, after a quick look, reached for a long boathook and thrust it over the side.

"Now!" whispered Jim, his mouth dry with excitement. He moved out from behind the capstan, ran lightly to the shadow of the ship's rail and moved quickly down the length of the ship. Just before he reached the stern he ducked behind a carriage gun. His three seamen fell in beside him.

"Wait until they start bringing the loot aboard," he warned. "Once they get their hands on that, they'll forget everything else."

One of the pirate crew gave a joyful shout and dragged a jute bag aboard. The others watched wide-eyed as he spilled the contents on deck. Gleaming silver, rich-looking in the yellow glow over the bay, held each eye. Suddenly their greed got the best of them. They dropped their weapons and leaned over the rail, their grasping hands reaching for more of the bags.

"Come on," Jim ordered.

The four Americans moved silently across the deck until they stood just behind the money-mad men.

"Turn around slowly and don't reach for your weapons," said Jim in a steady voice.

The men at the rail stiffened, then turned slowly to face the Americans. One evil-looking seaman glanced furtively at his cutlass on the deck.

Jim leveled his pistol at the man's chest. "If you're tired of living, try to pick it up!" he said in a steely voice. "Now turn around and face the rail."

One man hesitated too long to suit Hardy. He raised the heavy chain. The man turned quickly.

"Tie 'em up," Jim ordered his men. "Hands behind them."

Jim walked to the ship's side and called down to the relieved Moreau. "It's all over," he said. "You can come up now."

Angélique grabbed Jim's outstretched hand and climbed quickly up the side to the rail. She jumped to the deck and shouted gleefully, "Oh, Jim. You're taking your ship again!"

Jim smiled. "It was your plan that did it. We didn't even have to fight."

Angélique blushed and lowered her eyes. "You think maybe I am, as papa says, a wilful child."

Jim laughed. "You can be as wilful as you want, young lady, if you always come up with plans as good as this one."

"Jim!"

The midshipman heard Moreau's cry from the boat. He jumped the rail and saw the older man holding the boat alongside with difficulty. He grabbed the boathook and held the craft. "Come aboard, sir," he called down.

Moreau leaned over and picked up two remaining jute bags. "You want me to throw them in the bay?" he asked.

"Might as well take them along," answered Jim, with a grin. He motioned Hardy to take the bags.

When all his group was once again together, Jim called them to the stern, out of the prisoners' hearing. "We're not out of danger yet," he cautioned. "We're a

mighty small crew to man a ship this size." The thought
struck him that, if he could count Angélique, he actually
had one more than his original crew. "We can do it
though." He glanced aloft, then turned his face into the
slight breeze. "With a jib and the mains'l we ought to
be able to work clear of the bay."

"Aye, sir," replied Hews. "You want us to slip the
anchor?"

Jim looked toward the prisoners. "In a minute. First
I want to know why there are so few men aboard."

"Maybe Cruet and his men were taken by Dessalines'
army," said Moreau.

Jim shook his head. "He's too slippery for that."
He turned to Hews and Barnum. "Get one of the
prisoners. Get one that looks really scared."

A moment later the two seamen dragged a ragged-
looking pirate of Cruet's crew before the midshipman.

"They all look scared, sir," said Hews, contemptuously.

"Where's your captain?" Jim demanded of the prisoner. "Where's Cruet?"

The frightened prisoner rolled his eyes but refused to
answer.

Hardy took his length of chain and wrapped it around
the man's ankles. "Want me to throw him over the side,
Captain?" He grabbed the man by the arm.

"I talk! I talk!" screamed the pirate.

"Where is he?"

The prisoner, gesticulating wildly, launched into a
rapid-fire explanation in the patois of the island. Jim
couldn't understand him.

Moreau stepped up. "Cruet's probably in the longboat we saw. This scum says his captain is out on the
bay taking valuables from the refugees."

"That sounds like Cruet," said Hardy.

"We probably don't have too much time, then," said Jim. "No telling when Cruet will return. Take him back with the rest, Hardy." He turned to the other seamen. "Hoist the jib, slip the anchor and then hoist the mains'l. We'll get underway immediately."

With a speed that showed their years of experience, Jim's tiny crew soon had canvas on the ship. Slowly the brig filled away and began to move through the water. Jim took the helm, eyed the sails with satisfaction and set a course to clear the headland.

"Jim," Angélique plucked at the young officer's arm. "That boat. It seems to be coming after us very fast." She pointed astern.

Jim whirled and looked aft. A quarter of a mile away a longboat knifed toward the brig. He glanced over the side and saw that his ship was moving very slowly through the water. He darted another look at the pursuing boat and saw three flashing oars on each side. He glanced aloft. With this wind they could never outrun a well-manned longboat. Jim called Moreau and the three sailors aft.

"That longboat's after us," he said. "It seems the admiral wants his flagship back again." He pointed to the pivot gun on the stern. "Hews," he said to the gunner's mate, "let's discourage him. Break out powder and shot."

"Aye, sir," said Hews and ran to the hatchway.

"Hardy, you and Barnum gather up all the muskets you can find and bring 'em on deck."

The two sailors dashed away. Jim looked over his shoulder and thought the longboat had closed the distance slightly. Before them, the headland loomed dark on the starboard bow. If we can clear the point, he thought, they'll never catch us. A few well-laid shots should slow the pirates down. There wasn't much chance of Cruet getting the *Rover* back this time.

"Mr. Murdock!"

The midshipman heard Hews' shout and saw him running aft.

"Mr. Murdock," the gunner's mate panted, "there ain't a thimbleful of powder in the magazines!"

★

CHAPTER 17

Captain Murdock

"THAT can't be," Jim protested.

"It's the truth, sir. The whole magazine's been cleaned out," said Hews. "I don't figger it either, sir, but there ain't enough powder to prime a gun." Hardy and Barnum ran up at that moment and dropped a few cutlasses on deck. "No muskets below, sir. Looks like Cruet didn't trust his own crew none," said Barnum. "Not that I blame him," he muttered, as he looked over the prisoners huddled near the mast.

"There's no powder in the magazine, either," explained Hews to the two seamen.

"No powder?" cried Barnum. He shot a quick look at the longboat closing the gap steadily.

"This is bad, no?" said Moreau.

Jim gave Angélique a reassuring look. "Not too bad. We'll get more canvas on the ship. It may help, and after all, they have to board and there's five of us to beat them off." Five, he thought, against perhaps a dozen determined men, well-armed with pistols and cutlasses.

Hardy glanced at the ship's rail. "We could do with a few boarding nettings," he muttered.

"What did you say?" Jim asked sharply.

Hardy looked apologetically at his superior. "I just said, sir, we could use some boarding nettings."

166

"Take the helm, Hardy!" Jim cried, his face alight. "Hold her steady as she goes."

"Steady as she goes, sir," repeated Hardy, taking the wheel. He stared at the young officer, puzzled at the quick change that had come over him.

"The rest of you follow me!" Jim cried, and ran down the afterhatch to the captain's cabin.

When the others reached the cabin they stared in amazement at the midshipman. He was dragging the mattress off the captain's bunk.

"Here, help me," he shouted and slashed the lashings underneath with a knife. He reached down and hauled out a neatly folded fishing net and handed it to Hews. "Take it up on deck," he ordered. He handed Moreau and Barnum each a net, then picked up several boxes of fishing hooks and followed the other men topside.

"Spread 'em out here by the lee rail," he ordered. "Side by side." Jim turned to Angélique. "You can help, now." He handed her a box of hooks.

Angélique stared at the box in her hands.

"Look," explained Jim. He took a hook and attached it to the net with a quick twist. "Just put one every place the twine crosses," he said. "The more we get on, the better."

He turned to the two sailors. "Find some small stuff and lash the three nets together so that we have one big one."

Hews' eyes widened with understanding. "Yes, sir!" he shouted and ran to a small locker by the helm. "We'll catch ourselves a mess o' fish," he shouted to Hardy.

Jim twisted the hooks on the net as fast as he could. He saw that Angélique quickly mastered the technique. Her father grabbed a box and joined them.

When Hews and Barnum had finished their lashing,

Jim ordered them to find four long lines and tie them to the four corners of the large net. This completed, he ordered them to throw the other ends over the spanker gaff.

When all preparations were complete the net lay flat on deck, literally covered with cruelly barbed hooks.

"They'll board on the lee side," he said. "We'll let 'em too. When I give the order, haul on those lines for all you're worth." Astern, the longboat was not a hundred yards away. He could see the rise and fall of its oars in perfect unison and could hear Cruet screaming encouragement to his men.

"When they are alongside, lash the helm and get under cover," he said to Hardy.

The big helmsman acknowledged the order and reached for a coil of line on deck with one hand.

"The rest of you get behind the quarter guns and keep out of sight," said Jim. He handed each of the other three men the end of one line. "When I yell, haul taut and secure your end." He looked back at the approaching boat, "Keep down now. Lash that helm, Hardy, and stay under cover. He might get a lucky hit."

It's the waiting that's nerve-wracking, thought Jim, as he glanced around the deck anxiously. He almost wished now he could slow down the *Rover* and get the action over sooner. Cruet couldn't board except on the lee side. Jim hoped he was right in assuming he would try to board

on the quarter. If Cruet pushed on ahead to the waist, Jim knew he was in for trouble.

He waited tensely. The longboat's bow was now abreast the stern. He risked another look and saw Cruet, his face twisted in rage, standing in the boat with a pistol in each hand.

Suddenly, a bump against the brig's side electrified Jim and his companions. They saw hands clutch at the rail and watched the swarthy pirates swarm over the side.

For a moment the boarders hesitated, their eyes searching wildly for an enemy. Then began a grotesque dance, as those pirates who were barefooted began to leap in pain when the hooks sank into their flesh.

"Haul away!" yelled Jim at the top of his voice.

Suddenly the pirates watched a wall of netting rise on all sides of them. Frantically they lunged against the tough twine with curses of alarm. As the needle-sharp barbs dug into their flesh, their curses turned to screams of agony. The more they fought the hook-studded net, the more desperate their situation became. Finally they were so enmeshed they could not move without experiencing excruciating pain.

Jim and the others secured their lines and walked across the deck to stare at the net full of helpless pirates.

"A fine haul this, Mr. Murdock," laughed Hardy.

Jim sat on the edge of his chair. He let his eyes wander around the captain's cabin on the *Constitution*. The commodore had plenty of room to rattle around in. Compared to Jim's tiny cabin on the *Rover,* this space looked like a ballroom. Commodore Talbot had it fixed up nicely, too; curtains at the gallery windows, and solid mahogany furniture. Through one of the windows he could see the *Rover* riding at anchor astern of the great frigate. He couldn't help but wonder if he'd ever get aboard her again. He studied the senior officer sitting at the round table in the center of the room. Watching him turn the report, page by page, Jim was unable to decide whether the commodore believed him or not.

Jim glanced across the table and saw that both Moreau and Angélique were watching the commodore's face for his reaction. Angélique, a tiny frown on her brow, watched the commodore intently. She caught Jim's eye, smiled, and deliberately winked.

In spite of the seriousness of his present situation, Jim couldn't restrain a smile himself.

"Harumph!" Commodore Talbot cleared his throat and looked up from the report. "Most amazing. I might even say fantastic." He leveled his eyes on the midshipman. "Fortunately, sir, every word of your report has been verified by Mr. Moreau, and, ah—his charming daughter." He smiled and bowed slightly to Angélique. There was no smile on his face, however, when he returned his eyes to his young subordinate.

"Even so, Mr. Murdock, there are some points I must clear up." The commodore thumbed rapidly through the report.

Jim sat straighter and waited for the questions.

"This man Hardy," the commodore continued. "He actually struck an officer of the Navy?"

"Hardy was playing a game, sir," Jim answered. "He had to make it convincing. Cruet is a mighty shrewd scoundrel."

"He is supreme among all the pirates on Gonave?" asked the older officer.

"Well—" Jim hesitated. "I guess you could say that he finally attained that position when Rigaud promoted him to admiral. Actually, sir, I believe there are several

pirate strongholds along the coast, all similar to the one
Cruet commanded."

Commodore Talbot looked Jim straight in the eye.
"I must say your report is complete, Mr. Murdock. It
does much to clarify a rather damning charge submitted
by your captain." He cleared his throat again. "You
are aware, I take it, that Captain Mellon has returned
home on sick leave."

"Yes, sir," replied Jim.

"Lieutenant Knight now commands the *Victory*. His
report is—er—at variance with the previous commanding
officer's."

Jim remained silent. He risked another glance at the
two Moreaus and saw that both of them were regarding
him with faint smiles.

"In view of the more recent events," the squadron
commander continued, "I am therefore disregarding Captain Mellon's charges. You are restored to full duty, sir."
He closed the report. "I consider your actions in keeping
with the highest conduct of an officer and a gentleman."

For the first time, Jim breathed freely. "Thank you,
sir," he said.

"You will return to the *Rover* and resume command of
the prize. It is my intention to send her to the Navy
Agent at Charleston, South Carolina, for disposal."

"Aye, aye, sir," replied the midshipman, happily.

"And now, sir," said the senior officer, standing, "I pre-
sume you are anxious to return to your ship. The first
lieutenant will provide you with enough hands to augment
your small crew. I will arrange for imprisonment of
Cruet and his men aboard the *Constitution*."

Jim jumped to his feet as the commodore stood up.
"Thank you, sir. I will make preparations for getting
underway." He turned to Émile Moreau. He had hoped

to have more time with Angélique and her father before
he left. The three of them had shared so many experi-
ences he found it difficult to say good-by. He held out
his hand to the Creole. "Good-by, sir. I—"

"Mr. Murdock," the commodore broke in, "I neglected
to tell you that Mr. Moreau has requested passage for himself and his daughter to Charleston."

Jim turned to his senior in openmouthed astonishment.
The commodore, however, had his eyes on Angélique and
as the two of them exchanged smiles, Jim could have
sworn the girl actually winked at the older man.

"Well, Mr. Murdock," said the commodore, turning
to Jim again. "I trust the request will not inconvenience
you?"

"Holy—I mean, no, *sir!*" exclaimed Jim. He watched
Angélique move around the table to stand before him.

"You are very gracious, sir," Angélique said and
offered Jim her arm. "I will try to behave myself, *Captain* Murdock," she said with an impish glance.

Jim was aware of the two men's silent laughter as he
escorted Angélique from the cabin. He didn't care: all
he could think of was the long slow miles to Charleston.